BACK FROM THE GRAVE

A Jarvis House Mystery

BY

D1737427

SUZANNE FLOYD

COPYRIGHT

Cover by Bella Media Management

I dedicate this book to my husband Paul and our daughters, Camala and Shannon, and all my family. Thanks for all your support and encouragement.

"Once Lost, now found. Eternally thankful!" Our Daily Bread

CHAPTER ONE

Cady Townsend went blissfully through her life never wondering who her father was, never caring either. She wasn't the only one in her school without a dad. No one seemed to care one way or the other. Until the day she turned twenty-one. That was the day her life was turned upside down.

A limo was sitting in front of the small house Cady shared with her mom when she turned the corner onto the quiet street. Slowing down as she drove past, she tried to see past the dark windows to see who was inside. Other than the driver, she couldn't see anyone.

The only time she'd seen a limo in the small town where she grew up was when the funeral home drove the family of a recently deceased person to the cemetery. Her heart did a little tap dance in her chest. Had something happened to her mom? Why hadn't anyone called her? Who would call the funeral home? Didn't they send a hearse instead of a limo?

Pulling into the driveway, she jumped out of her car almost before it stopped running. "Mom, Mom." She ran up the walk to the house. Twisting the doorknob, she pushed on the door at the same time. Instead of opening, her shoulder struck solid wood. The door was locked. Her heart was in her throat now. In a town the size of Tumbleweed, Arizona, no one bothered to lock their doors. Her hands were shaking so much it took three tries before she could fit the key into the lock.

Finally getting the door open, she rushed inside. "Mom, where are you? Are you all right?" Everything in the living room looked normal. Nothing was out of place and her mom was sitting in her chair rocking gently.

"Yes, Dear, I'm fine. Happy birthday. I hope you had a good day." She had the same gentle smile on her lips that Cady had seen every day of her life.

"Thank you, my day was..." She shook her head. "Never mind that. Why is there a limo out front? Why was the door locked?" A frown drew her dark brows together. "What's going on?" As her fear began to subside her knees threatened to give out. Sinking onto the couch before she fell down, she took her mom's hand.

Olivia took a steadying breath, letting it out slowly. "I locked the door because I didn't want that man to come in until you got home. I wanted a chance to explain."

"Explain what? What man? Who's out there?" Her heart was in her throat. Olivia knew who was in the limo and his presence required an explanation. This couldn't be good. "Are you sick, Mom?"

Olivia gave a little laugh. "Not in any way physical. Just give me a minute to explain." She looked out the window. The driver had just opened the back door for the man inside to step out. She was running out of time.

Cady's gaze followed her mom's. A tall man in his late forties or early fifties stood beside the limo looking toward the house. She couldn't see his face clearly, but something about him seemed familiar.

"He's your father. He's come to see you." The words tumbled out in a rush.

"My father?" Cady's head began to swim. "I don't have a father."

"Of course you do, my dear. Everyone has a father." She grinned at her daughter's statement.

"I know that, but I've never seen him before. You never said anything about my dad. I just assumed..." She stopped. She didn't know what she'd assumed. They had never talked about her dad or why he wasn't around. "I guess I assumed he was dead."

"Well, yes, when you never asked about him, I let you believe that. But he isn't dead." She drew in a sharp breath as the man started toward the door. "He said it was time for you to know him." Olivia's hands were shaking. It had been more than twenty-one years since she'd seen him. She always knew he was in the background, but he never approached her or

2

Cady. It was the only way he could protect them. But to show up like this... She shook her head. She didn't know what to expect.

"He never cared enough to see me before, why now?"

"It wasn't that he didn't care. It was better that way."

"Better for who?" The doorbell rang, cutting off her words.

When neither of them went to answer the door, the bell rang again. "What am I supposed to do?" Cady whispered.

Olivia lifted her thin shoulders, letting them droop. "Open the door."

Cady shook her head, her chin-length dark hair falling across her face. "No," she whispered.

The bell rang for the third time accompanied by several sharp knocks on the door. He was getting impatient. "Olivia, please open the door." Instead of waiting for her to invite him in, he opened the door himself. Standing on the threshold, he took several minutes to stare at Cady before entering the room.

"You've grown into a beautiful young woman," he finally spoke.

His words came to her as through a tunnel. Her head was spinning. This couldn't be happening. He could be anywhere from forty to sixty. His hair was as dark as Cady's was. There were only a few grey streaks at the temples. His dark eyes roamed over her seated figure. He was tall and looked like he worked out regularly. She knew why he looked familiar. She saw those eyes every morning in the mirror. There was little doubt they were related, but he couldn't be her father. He was supposed to be dead.

He took several steps toward her, and she abruptly stood up. "Stay right there. Don't come any closer." She held out her hands as though warding off a blow. "I don't know you. You have no right coming here like this."

Olivia stood up, taking Cady's hand. "His name is Mason Jarvis. He's your..."

3

"Don't say it." Cady's sharp tone stopped her mom from finishing the statement. "We might be biologically related, but he isn't my dad. A dad wouldn't show up out of the blue twenty-one years after his daughter was born."

"That was the only way to protect both of you." His voice was deep and well-modulated.

"Where have you been for the last twenty-one years? Were you in prison? Are you on the run from the law? Are you a mobster? What?"

The man chuckled at that. "No, I'm not a mobster and I'm not running from the law. I haven't been in prison either." He sighed. "If it were only that simple."

Cady turned to her mother. "What's he talking about?"

"It's a rather long story."

"You've had twenty-one years to tell me. Why wait until now?"

"Can I at least come in and sit down so we can talk?" He took two more steps.

She retreated the same two steps. "No, you can't. I don't have anything to say to you." She looked at her mom. "How could you spring something like this on me? Happy Birthday, you have a dad? Well, this birthday present is being returned. Go back to wherever it is you came from and leave me alone." With that, Cady took a wide path around him and stormed out of the house, slamming the door behind her.

Driving away from the house she grew up in, the only home she'd ever known, she had no destination in mind. She only wanted to get as far away as possible. How could her mom betray her like this? How could he simply walk into her life like it was the most natural thing in the world? Where had he been all these years?

When her phone rang, she ignored it. She didn't want to talk to anyone, especially her mom or … She paused. She couldn't remember what her mom said his name was. How weird was it that she'd never asked about the man who had provided half of her DNA? She knew nothing about him. All these years, she hadn't even been curious. Why was that?

She'd lived her entire life in Tumbleweed, in northern Arizona. Her mom taught at the small school in town. Cady had what some would consider a picture-perfect life. She'd never lacked for love. There simply hadn't been the need or the room in her life for a father.

After her phone rang for the third time, she pulled it from her purse. It was Mom again. This time she turned her phone off. She wasn't ready to talk to anyone, especially her mom.

It was beginning to get dark when she remembered she had a date. Robert was taking her to dinner for her birthday. They were planning on going back to her house for cheesecake with her mom later. "Well, that's not going to happen," she muttered. As long as that man was there, she wasn't going back. She felt slightly childish, but she couldn't help it. Anyone would be shocked to learn they had a father after believing he was dead for twenty-one years.

Pulling into the parking lot in front of the grocery store, she took out her phone. It was almost too late to cancel their date. Robert would be going to the house in a matter of minutes. She didn't want him stepping into the mess that her life had suddenly become. Until she could figure it out, she couldn't explain it to anyone else. What would he think about a father turning up at this late date? Probably the same thing she thought: Too little too late.

"Hi, Robert, I'm sorry for the late notice," she began as soon as he answered his phone. "But something's come up and I'm going to have to cancel our date."

"Really? Did you get a better offer from some guy with a limo?" His tone was angry.

"What? Where are you?"

"I'm sitting in front of your house looking at a fancy

stretch limo. Who else are you seeing?"

"No one." She was confused. He'd never acted jealous before. They didn't have that type of relationship. "Look, I'm sorry. Things are very complicated tonight. I don't feel up to explaining right now. I'm not in the mood to celebrate anything. I'll try to explain later." *Or maybe not,* she thought. Did he deserve an explanation after this little display? She didn't think so.

"Really." His voice dripped with disdain. "That's all you have to say after standing me up? You really think I'm going to be willing to carry on with our relationship after you dump me for some rich guy?"

"I'm not dumping you for anyone. I don't know where this is coming from, but you don't know what you're talking about." He was stepping on the last of her already frayed nerves.

"Then why don't you explain? Whose limo is sitting in front of your house? Where are you?"

She took a calming breath, letting it out slowly. "As I said, it's complicated."

"You owe me an explanation after standing me up," he pressed. "I've been planning this for a month. And you won't explain. What else am I supposed to think?"

Now she was confused. They hadn't known each other much longer than a month. How could he have been planning their date that long? Their relationship was more one of friendship than boyfriend and girlfriend. She didn't understand why he was so angry. She didn't need this, not tonight.

"I'm sorry, Robert, really I am. I don't want to get into this tonight." That was certainly the truth. Was she even going home? *Not if that man was still there,* she silently answered. She wasn't even sure if she wanted to talk to her mom right now.

"So you are seeing someone else." It wasn't a question.

"No, that's not what I said. I don't know why you're so upset."

"Well, you're cancelling our date at the very last minute. How do you think I feel about finding a limo sitting in front of your house when I come here to pick you up? What am I supposed to think?"

"Maybe you could think it's complicated like I said."

"That isn't an explanation, Cady, that's a cop-out."

"Fine, you want an explanation. How's this? The father I thought was dead put in an appearance for the first time in my life. He thinks I should be okay with that. How's that for an explanation? I'm sorry if it isn't enough, but it's the only explanation you're going to get. Good-bye." He was sputtering something when she ended the call.

Before she could turn her phone off, it rang again. A picture of her mom popped up on the screen. She declined the call and turned her phone off. She wasn't ready to talk to her yet. Having a dad she knew nothing about wasn't a good surprise. She didn't know how either of them could expect her to be happy with this.

Resting her head on the back of the seat, she tried to sort out her feelings. What was wrong with Robert? He'd never acted possessive or jealous before. Why now? What did he mean he'd been planning this for a month? That was about the time they'd met. Their dates had been casual, there was nothing serious between them.

Robert Gates had moved to Tumbleweed when he took the job of manager of the recently opened hotel in town about a month ago. They met when he came into the library where she was head librarian looking for information on the area.

He'd asked her out for coffee on the pretext that he wanted to learn more about the town and the people living here. He'd seemed interested and interesting. She hadn't been seeing anyone at the time, and when he asked her out for dinner, she saw no reason to turn him down. Since then they went out to dinner once or twice a week.

He'd been a little disappointed at Tumbleweed's lack of an exciting nightlife. Hiking in the forest wasn't his idea of fun, but he had agreed to go hiking with her several times. You didn't have to go to a bar to have fun. There were plenty of other things to do.

She hadn't considered him her boyfriend, just a friend. She thought he felt the same way about her. She had insisted on paying for dinner once or twice and he hadn't objected. Did that sound like something a boyfriend did? She shook her head. So where did this jealousy come from?

After his little temper tantrum, she didn't even want to be friends any longer. This wasn't a good time for the green-eyed monster to rear its ugly head. She'd had enough surprises for one day. She certainly didn't need any more complications right now.

She shook her head. Robert's hurt feelings were the least of her worries at the moment. There were more important matters on her mind.

Instead of going home, she headed for Blair's apartment. Blair Ratcliff had been her best friend all through school. They had been roommates as well in college. Cady studied Library Science and Blair became a nurse. When they graduated, they both moved back to Tumbleweed. They had always shared their deepest secrets. More than anyone she knew, Blair would understand now why she was upset.

"Cady, hi, happy birthday." Blair was surprised to see her friend. Giving Cady a hug, she stepped back. "What are you doing here? Don't you have a date with Robert?"

"That boat sailed and it sank. I don't think I'll be seeing him again."

"What did he do?" Her gaze traveled over Cady looking for signs that she was injured. "If he hurt you, you need to call the police."

"No, he didn't do anything like that. He's just a jerk." She sighed softly. "Do you have any wine?"

"Do bears poop in the woods?" Blair laughed. "Of course I have wine."

Cady followed her into the small kitchen sitting down at the table. Did she begin this conversation with the man she'd always thought was dead showing up or Robert's jealous accusation that she was seeing someone else? She shook her head.

Blair placed a glass of wine in front of her before taking a seat. "Okay. What's going on?" If Robert did something to her friend, she'd make him regret it. The few times she had been around Robert, she thought there was something off with him. He kept the relationship casual, but he also wanted to take up all of her free time. She'd never said anything to Cady. Maybe she should have.

"It's not just Robert, but I won't be seeing him again." She shrugged "We are… were just friends. I thought he felt the same way. But he accused me of cheating on him."

Blair frowned. "Why would he think that?"

"Because of the fancy limo in front of my house. He thought I was dumping him for some rich guy."

"Wait a minute. A limo? Who has a limo in Tumbleweed?"

Drawing a deep breath, Cady released it slowly. "Apparently my dad does. He showed up today." She blurted it out.

"Huh?" Blair's mouth dropped open. "I thought your dad was dead."

"Yeah, so did I. It seems that my mom has been lying to me all these years." She sighed. "Actually, she didn't lie. She just never said anything about him. Maybe it's my fault because I never asked. It didn't seem like a big deal that I didn't have a dad. You don't have a dad." Blair's dad died in a car accident when the girls were five years old. "I guess when your dad died I assumed that was why I didn't have a dad. Mom never mentioned him."

"Did your mom know he was alive? What did she say when he showed up?"

"He's your father," she said, making air quotes around the words. "She said it was time I knew him."

"Just like that? Where has he been for the last twenty-one years?"

Cady shrugged. "Your guess is as good as mine. I didn't stick around to ask questions."

"What are you going to do? He doesn't want you to go live with him, does he?" It was horrifying to think about living with someone you just met.

"Hell no!" Cady exclaimed. "Sorry." She sighed again. "I don't know what either of them was thinking. He said it was for my protection that he waited until now to meet me." Angry tears burned the back of her eyes.

"Your protection? Why would you need to be protected and from whom? Is he some kind of criminal running from the law?"

Cady gave a harsh chuckle. "I actually asked him that. I'm not sure if he was offended or thought it was funny. But I guess he isn't a mobster or running from the law."

"So who was he protecting you from?"

Cady shrugged. "I didn't stick around long enough to find that out. I stormed out of the house after Mom dropped that bombshell on me. I don't know how long I drove around trying to make sense of what had happened. I forgot all about Robert taking me out for my birthday until minutes before he was supposed to pick me up. When I called to cancel, he got upset. That's when he accused me of seeing someone else."

"Why would he do that? You haven't been dating that long.

Did you explain about your... that man?"

"Not right away. I didn't want to get into it with him. I told him something came up at home. He was upset that I was cancelling at the last minute." She frowned. "He said he'd been planning this for a month."

"Isn't that about the time the two of you met?" Blair asked.

Cady nodded, her dark hair swinging around her face. "I don't know where he got the idea he'd been planning it for a month. I tried to tell him things were complicated, but he wouldn't let it go. He wanted to know if I was seeing someone else."

Shaking her head, she shrugged. "We've never talked about anything personal. He's met Mom when he came to pick me up, but that's all. He never asked me about my dad or any other family. I don't know anything about his family either. We don't... didn't have that kind of relationship."

She paused. "Come to think of it, whenever I asked about his family, he would give me a short answer and change the subject." She sighed again. "Anyway, I gave him the Cliff Notes version of what happened and hung up." She lifted one shoulder, letting it drop. There were too many other things happening in her life, she didn't want to think about Robert.

"What are you going to do about... you know? Maybe you should talk to your mom and see why she never said anything until now."

"Not tonight." Cady shook her head. "I'm so upset with her, I'm afraid I'll say something I can't take back. I guess I can always sneak in through my bedroom window like I did when I was a kid. She'd never know I was there." Both girls started laughing. It felt good to let go of the tension that had been riding her shoulders since she got home from work.

"That would be something to see. Can you still climb that old tree?"

"What? It's not like I'm ninety or something. It's been a

while, but I'm sure I can still do it."

"I have a better idea. You stay here tonight. That way you won't risk breaking an arm or leg falling out of the tree. Things will look better in the morning. We'll figure out something then." She had her fingers crossed it was the truth. "We still wear the same size clothes. You can wear something of mine tomorrow." At five feet eight, Cady was five inches taller than Blair. "The pants and skirts might be a little short on you though," she said with a laugh.

It took a long time for Cady to fall asleep once they finished the bottle of wine and dissected her relationship with Robert. By mutual consent, they had avoided further talk of the news her mom had dropped on her head. She needed to sort through her feelings before she talked to her mom. *Happy Birthday to me,* she thought as she laid there in the dark. *What am I supposed to do now?* With that thought, sleep claimed her.

CHAPTER TWO

"Why didn't you stop her from leaving?" Mason glared across the room at Olivia.

"What did you expect me to do? She's a grown woman. It isn't like I can tell her to go to her room for misbehaving." Olivia was still sitting in her chair. It was like she'd taken root and couldn't move. "How did you think she was going to react? You can't expect her to welcome you with open arms when she's believed for twenty-one years that you were dead. That was the way you wanted it. The way it had to be."

"Not *dead*," he contradicted, sounding slightly shocked at the idea. His long legs carried him across the room in three strides. Flopping down on the couch where Cady had been sitting just moments ago, he rested his head on the back cushion. "I thought you'd tell her that we were divorced or something."

"Or something is right. We were never married. How do you think Cady would have felt if I'd told her that?" There was no rancor in her voice. She'd accepted what happened a long time ago. There was no use raking it over the coals now. "By the way, I'm sorry for your loss. How are your kids taking their mother's death?"

He shrugged. "They are both naturally upset, Jerrod more so than Melanie. She and Belinda hadn't been close for a long time. She is the image of her mother, inside and out."

Olivia took that to mean she was beautiful on the outside and mean as a snake on the inside. She kept that thought to herself. Why rub salt in an open wound?

"I suppose it would have been easier on both of them if I was the one to die."

Olivia gasped. "Why would you even say that? You're their father. They love you."

13

"I'm not so sure of that last part. Belinda had turned them against me years ago. Although they didn't always get along with their mother I think they loved her in their own way. I'm not sure what their feelings for me are." He shrugged. "It is what it is."

Olivia thought she had played a part in that. If she hadn't fallen in love with Mason and gotten pregnant, he might have been able to patch things up with his kids if not with his wife. Their relationship had been strained long before she came along. It was too late for that now.

"What are we going to do about Cady? Do you know where she went? If I could just talk to her, it might help."

Oliva shook her head. "She had a date tonight. I'm not sure if she cancelled after she left here. I think she turned her phone off. She was rather upset." That was an understatement. Her daughter had been furious with both of them. She sighed. As Mason said, it is what it is.

"They were going to come back here after dinner for cake." A warm blush crept over her cheeks. "I know birthday cake sounds like a kid's party, but it isn't just a cake. Cady loves my cheesecake. I was planning on putting twenty-one candles in it for her."

She paused for a moment, avoiding eye contact with him. "Since you didn't come here after your wife died, I thought you had decided to leave things as they were. I wasn't expecting you to show up today, on her birthday of all days." In actuality, she'd been hoping he had forgotten this was Cady's birthday. She should have known better. Mason had a memory like an elephant. He forgot very little. He had always remembered when his daughter was born. Each year he would send enough money that she could afford to take her somewhere special during the summer when school was out.

He also remembered Olivia's birthday. Every year a dozen red roses were delivered on her birthday. She had always told

Cady that she bought them herself. There was never a note or card, but she knew Mason had sent them.

Although she had never asked for child support, money was deposited in her account every month. She'd saved that for Cady's college, but that hadn't been necessary. He had paid her tuition as well. She'd told Cady one of the scholarships she'd applied for had been approved.

Olivia knew he had followed their lives even though he never personally contacted either of them. That had also been part of their agreement. Her little white lies were beginning to catch up with her.

"When did you think I would come to see her?" he asked mildly, breaking in on all the memories that were flooding her mind. "Were you hoping that I had forgotten about her? About you?" he added softly. Before she could respond, he continued. "I know almost as much about her as you do." He held his head up as though he was proud of his subterfuge.

"What are you talking about?" Olivia's heart was pounding in her chest. "You agreed not to contact her or me after..." She couldn't finish her sentence.

"I'm sorry. I couldn't help myself. She is my daughter. I might not have been able to attend as many sporting events as you, but I was there for several games. As long as there was a threat, I made sure someone was watching out for you both all these years. I was even able to congratulate her when she graduated from college."

Olivia gasped, and he patted her hand. "Don't worry, she didn't know who I was. I told her I was the father of one of her classmates. With that large of a graduating class, she never knew the difference."

She narrowed her eyes at him. "Why did you do that? You were taking a big risk. We both agreed you wouldn't contact her until..." Her words trailed off. It sounded terrible to say they were waiting for his wife to die.

15

He shrugged his broad shoulders. "I didn't contact her. I wanted to see her graduate. Do you blame me for that? I wasn't expecting to be able to talk to her, but when the opportunity presented itself I wasn't going to turn away." He sighed. "We only spoke for a few minutes, but it was enough to know she is a wonderful young woman. So unlike my other children." The words were an indictment against them.

"What about them?" Olivia asked softly. "Cady's shock is nothing compared to what your other children will feel if you spring a younger sister on them so soon after their mother's death."

"I'm certain they are both aware they had a half-sister. Belinda knew of Cady. Although we hadn't been living as man and wife for several years when you and I met, she was still my wife. She took every opportunity to remind me of that fact. She took great pleasure in destroying any relationship I hoped to have with Jerrod and Melanie. She never passed up a chance to let them know that I had been unfaithful." His voice was bitter.

He wished as he had so many times over the years, that he had gotten a divorce and married Olivia. Belinda would never agree to a divorce though. She would have destroyed him financially and socially. What did it say about him that he cared more about money and his reputation than the woman he loved and their child?

But it wasn't only for himself that he'd stayed. Belinda would also have made sure that Olivia and Cady paid as well. He hadn't been willing to risk that. He'd already done enough to hurt them. As long as he stayed away, Belinda refrained from harming them in any way.

When the clock above the mantle chimed ten o'clock and Cady and Robert hadn't stopped for cheesecake, Olivia knew Cady wasn't coming home that night. "Do you think she went home with the young man she had dinner with?" Mason frowned. He couldn't dictate whether she slept with someone, but he hoped she wouldn't simply because she was upset about him. "Is their relationship such that she is already sleeping with him?"

Olivia shook her head. "I don't think Cady feels that way about Robert. He's a friend, that's all." She hoped that was the case, but she had no idea what her daughter would do after what they had dropped on her. She had been so upset when she introduced Mason as her father. She'd given up calling her after more than a half dozen calls that went straight to voice mail.

"Where would she go? Is she waiting for me to leave?"

There was hurt in his voice, but Olivia couldn't help that. Springing him on her this way had been a monumental mistake. "She probably went to see Blair Ratcliff. They have been friends since they were little. When either of them is upset about something, they always turn to the other one for comfort."

"So why haven't you called this friend? We need to make sure she's all right. Anything can happen to a young woman alone after dark."

Olivia laughed at that. "This isn't New York City or Chicago or even Los Angeles where the crime rate is soaring. Tumbleweed is a safe place to live. Why don't you go to the hotel for the night? We can try this again tomorrow. I'm sure your chauffeur is tired of waiting outside by now. We should have asked him to come inside a long time ago." She hadn't even thought of the man sitting outside all this time.

"I told him to go to the hotel if I didn't come right back out." He chuckled. "I didn't think Cady would take off like that. I suppose I was hoping she would be more receptive to meeting me." He sighed. "I'll text Bill now so he can come pick me up."

~~~

17

Cady groaned when sunlight filtered around the edges of the blinds the next morning. Rolling over, she picked up her phone. She hadn't bothered to turn it back on when she went to bed. It was only five o'clock. *I guess five hours of sleep isn't bad after the birthday surprise last night,* she thought. Not everyone gets a dad as a birthday present. Her head was still spinning with that piece of news. Everything that had happened felt surreal.

There were more calls from her mom and even some from Robert. She deleted them without listening to the messages. She wasn't ready to talk to either of them. She wasn't sure she'd ever be ready to talk to Robert again. He'd been way out of line. It had never crossed her mind that he was getting serious. He never acted as though he thought of her as anything but a friend. She was eventually going to have to talk to her mom, but not right now.

Pushing herself up, she went into the kitchen to start the coffee. She didn't have to be at the library for another four hours. Going back to sleep for a few more hours would be nice, but it would be impossible to shut off her mind now. Why had her mom lied to her all these years? They said it was to protect her? Protect her from whom?

While she was growing up, she'd never questioned the fact that Olivia seldom went out. Yes, she occasionally went to dinner with different men, but she never let it go any further than an occasional dinner. Why? Was she still in love with this man?

Some people only fall in love once in their life. Is that what had happened to Olivia? If that was the case, why weren't they together? Why hadn't he ever come around while she was growing up? Her mind was spinning with questions. Had they gotten divorced and Olivia had been carrying a torch for him all these years? Nothing was making any sense

Another thought popped into her head and she sat down

before she fell down. Maybe they were never married. Even worse, was he married and she was the result of an affair? *What does that make me?* she thought. *A love child*, she silently answered, preferring that description to a more literal one. *Why had Mom waited until now to tell me? Why was he here now?*

Questions plagued her. The only way she was going to get the answers she needed was to confront her mom. She wasn't ready to see... She wished she could remember the name Olivia had called him. She shook her head. After being told he was her father everything else had disappeared from her mind.

The thought of facing him caused her stomach to roll. She had no idea what she would even say to him. *Hi Dad. Where have you been all my life?* Giving a small laugh, she shook her head. That was almost as ridiculous as the way he had been introduced to her.

She didn't know what she was going to do about Robert either. She'd never considered him anything more than a friend. She always thought he felt the same. Yes, they went out to dinner, but they took turns paying. What man who is serious about a woman does that? She'd never considered that he was serious about her.

He'd never shown any signs of being jealous until last night. Heck, they hadn't progressed beyond a simple kiss on the cheek when he picked her up or brought her home. They didn't even hold hands. His actions the night before had been totally off the rails.

She was still sitting at the kitchen table when Blair wandered out of her bedroom an hour later. "You're up rather early after our late night. Still, thinking about what to say to your mom? Or are you thinking about how you're going to kick Robert to the curb?" She gave a soft chuckle.

"Oh, I don't have to think about that. If he didn't get the message when I ignored his calls and texts, I guess I'll have to make things a little clearer. As for Mom…" She shrugged. "I don't have any idea what to say to her."

"Let her do all the talking," Blair suggested. "I'm sure she has quite a story to tell."

"I'll say," Cady agreed. "But I can't think of any excuse why she would keep this sort of thing from me and then spring it on me the way they did." She shook her head. "It's almost unforgivable." She was getting angry all over again. "I've tried to figure out what happened, and I've come to the conclusion that they were never married, at least not to each other. That makes me illegitimate. He's married. Or he was." Sighing, she shrugged. "Why else wouldn't he have visited me while I was growing up?"

Blair shrugged. "That doesn't carry the stigma it used to. No one pays attention to that anymore."

Cady thought about that for a minute, then nodded. "I guess you're right. It just feels weird. Do you think on some level I knew that? Maybe that's why I never pressed mom about my father."

"Being illegitimate doesn't change who you are. You're still the same person."

"Yeah, I guess." Cady shrugged.

"So what are you going to do?"

Cady sighed. "I need to talk to Mom, but I don't want to talk to him. Not yet anyway. I want to hear what she has to say first."

"Sounds like a solid plan." Blair nodded in agreement. "Now, let's figure what you're going to wear to work today." She chuckled. "Do you want high-water pants or a mini skirt?"

"Maybe I should just wait until Mom leaves for school. I can go home to shower and change into fresh clothes." Her heart began to pound at the idea of possibly running into… him. It would be a long while before she could think of him as her dad, maybe not ever. She wished she could remember his name.

"I could always call in sick and spend the day relaxing here." One eyebrow arched up when she looked at her friend hoping she would agree.

"Relaxing or hiding out?" Blair asked.

"Okay." Cady sighed. "I'll go to work, but if he comes into the library, I'm not going to talk to him. Can you imagine what the gossips would do with this juicy topic?" She shuddered at the thought.

She enjoyed living in the small town, but there were drawbacks. One of which was the busybodies always whispering behind your back while pretending to be your friend. What would she do if he came to the library? Having a hushed argument with the library patrons listening in wasn't something she wanted.

"Go take a shower." Blair pulled her out of the chair. "Then we'll try to find something in my closet that will fit those long legs." She chuckled at the idea of Cady facing those same busybodies who frequented the library daily wearing a skirt three inches too short.

CHAPTER THREE

Robert was leaning against his car when Cady pulled into the parking lot at the library shortly before nine. Before she had even shut off the engine, he opened the door for her. "What are you doing here, Robert?" she asked coldly.

"I came to apologize for last night." He reached for her hand. When she pulled back, he took a step away from her, allowing her to stand up. "I'm hoping you can forgive me."

"There's nothing to forgive," she replied in the same cold tone. He gave an exaggerated sigh of relief. "I would like you to answer a question for me though." When he nodded, there was a cautious look in his eyes. "What did you mean when you said you'd been planning last night for a month? We had barely met a month ago."

"Oh, um," he stammered, "I knew from the moment I saw you that you were the woman of my dreams." He nodded his head eagerly.

"Is that so?" He nodded again. "Then why has it taken you so long to even hold my hand, not to mention giving me a proper kiss good night."

"I didn't want to rush you. I wanted to show you how I felt first."

Yeah, right, she thought. "Well, most men don't let the "woman of their dreams"," she made air quotes around the words, "pick up the check for dinner."

"Again, I thought I was being considerate. I didn't think modern women expected men to always pick up the tab."

Cady shook her head. He had an answer for everything. "Do you think modern women enjoy being accused of stepping out on someone they are casually dating?"

"Casually dating? I thought we were getting serious."

"Whatever gave you that impression? We barely know

each other."

"Well, I was serious. If I wasn't moving fast enough for you, you could have said something. If you wanted to sleep with me, I would have been happy to oblige. Can we start over? I want to show you how much I care for you." He took a step toward her and she held up her hand in a stop gesture.

She couldn't believe he would say something like that. "No, that isn't going to happen. Now if you'll excuse me. I need to get to work. The library is about ready to open." She sailed off without a backward glance.

Once inside, she released the breath she'd been holding. At least he hadn't followed her to continue their argument. How had she ever considered him a nice guy?

For the next hour, she watched every time the door opened to make sure Robert didn't come in. She said a prayer that... She frowned trying to remember the man's name. Was she so desperate to forget what Olivia had said, that had blocked his name from her mind? Whatever, she was praying that he didn't come in while she was at work. That would be the ultimate humiliation.

Just after lunch, the local Ladies Book Club came in for the weekly meeting. The group of widows met at the library every Friday to discuss the previous week's book choice and to pick a new one. Instead of making their way to the back of the library where they always met, they headed straight for her desk.

"Good afternoon, Cady." Isabell Brewster was the spokeswoman for the group. She was also the biggest gossip in town. "Did you have a nice birthday dinner last night?" A smirk lifted the corners of her thin lips.

"Hello, Ladies. Yes, I had a nice birthday." She almost choked on the lie. "Thank you. Blair and I always have a good time when we're together."

"Blair?" The woman frowned. "We," *Meaning she,* Cady

thought, "saw that nice limousine out in front of your house last night. We assumed Robert had rented it for a special occasion." Again she used the royal we when she really meant she had assumed Robert rented the limo. She pointedly looked at Cady's left hand. They all seemed disappointed that her ring finger was bare. "We couldn't help but notice the limo was parked in the hotel parking lot all night."

"Is that right?" Cady put on her most innocent look. "I wasn't aware of that. Do you need help finding a new book to dissect, um review this week?" She changed the subject. Just because they were being nosy, didn't mean she had to rise to the bait.

Robert wasn't the only one interested in who was in that limo. She wasn't going to give them the satisfaction of filling them in. She wished she hadn't told Robert as much as she had the night before. Would he feed the gossips with what she'd told him? It would hurt her mom as much as it would hurt her if he did.

"Oh, no, of course not. We already have the next book picked out. We're all glad you had a nice time." There were looks of disappointment all around as they walked away.

Chalk one up for me, she thought. There was nothing better to lift their spirits than some juicy gossip. They weren't malicious; at least most of them weren't. They just loved to know everyone else's business.

By the end of the day, Cady was exhausted. After the way her birthday ended, she hadn't slept well the night before. Her stomach was twisted in knots at the thought of the conversation she was going to have with her mom. Before going home though, she was going to make sure there were no more surprises. If *he* was going to be there, she'd spend the night at Blair's again.

"Cady, are you all right?" Olivia answered the phone on the first ring. "I'm so sorry about how last night turned out.

It's my fault. Please come home so we can talk this out."

"Is he going to be there?" Cady couldn't stop the cold tone from creeping into her voice.

"No, dear." Olivia sighed. "It will be just the two of us. But you do need to talk to Mason at some point."

That's his name. She tried to remember his last name, but that still eluded her. It didn't matter. She wasn't going to be talking to him any time soon. At least she hoped she wasn't. "I'd like a few answers before that happens. I think you owe me that much." Her voice was harsher than she'd intended.

Normally, Olivia would call her on it, but not today. She knew she had it coming. Both she and Mason were complicit in the way they'd handled things. "Are you coming home tonight?"

For several heartbeats, Cady debated what she was going to say. Giving a sigh, she answered. "Yes, I'm leaving work now. I'll be there in a few minutes." That was one of the advantages of living in a small town. Everything was only minutes away. It was also a disadvantage when you needed time to figure out what you were going to say. She'd had all day and still didn't know, so a few more minutes wouldn't help.

The street was empty when she turned the corner, and she breathed a sigh of relief. She didn't want to think her mom would blindside her two days in a row. Olivia was sitting in the same spot she'd been the night before when Cady opened the door. "Hi, Mom." She was almost afraid of saying anything else.

"Hello, Dear. I'm so sorry about how last night turned out. I didn't know he was going to show up until he was here." The words tumbled out as soon as she saw her daughter. Drawing a deep breath, she let it out slowly. "Did you go out with Robert as planned?" She was also having a hard time trying to figure out what to say.

When Cady shook her head, her dark hair fell across her eye. Pushing it behind her ear, she sighed. "That didn't turn out as planned either. But he isn't who we need to talk about. Why didn't you ever tell me my father was alive? Why did you let me think he was dead?" Those were the first questions she wanted answered. The rest would come later.

Olivia seemed to shrink in stature as she sat there. "You were never curious or asked questions. It was easier to let you assume he was dead."

"Well, we both know what assuming does. I want to know why you never told me the truth." Cady was having trouble keeping her tone civil as she began to get angry all over again.

Olivia shrugged. "It was easier than trying to explain to a small child that her mother was an adulterer." Tears sparkled in her blue eyes.

"You didn't have to use that term," Cady stated. "I wouldn't have even known what that meant. Because Blair's dad died in that accident, I assumed my dad was dead as well. The parents of other kids in school were divorced and they still saw both of their parents. Since my father never came to see me, I figured he was dead. Why did he turn up yesterday of all days?"

Olivia shrugged. "I haven't spoken to him in more than twenty-one years. I didn't know he was going to show up on our doorstep. He felt that he'd waited twenty-one years to meet you. He didn't want to wait any longer."

"But you knew it was him even before he came to the door?"

Olivia nodded. "I wanted time to explain who he was before you met him. He didn't give me that chance. I am so sorry," she whispered, tentatively reaching out for her daughter's hand. When Cady didn't pull away, she gripped her hand tightly. "I am so sorry," she repeated. "For everything. I should have told you about Mason years ago but I couldn't.

When you never asked about your father, I simply let it go."

"Why couldn't you tell me? What did he mean he was protecting us?"

Olivia sighed. It was time to tell the whole sordid story. "I met Mason right after I graduated from college. He hired me to tutor his son and daughter."

"I have a brother and sister?" Cady interrupted. The shocks kept coming.

"Yes, Jerrod was eight years old at the time and Melanie was four. At the ripe old age of eight, he had already been expelled from two private schools. His mother wouldn't have him going to a public school. Even at that young age, they were both totally out of control. Melanie would have tantrums when she didn't get her way on anything. That was why Mason hired me as their tutor. He was hoping I would be able to instill some discipline in them. It didn't happen."

She sighed, her eyes taking on a distant expression as she looked into the past. "After meeting his wife I understood why. She was as out of control as they were. She might have been bipolar or something." She shook her head. "Truthfully, she was simply a hateful person."

With another sigh, Olivia looked at her daughter. "Mason tried to deal with his wife and children, but nothing he said made any difference. We spent a lot of time together trying to find a way to deal with what was happening with the children." She lifted her shoulders, letting them drop. "He was very unhappy in his marriage. Because of everything that was happening at home, his business was suffering.

"I felt sorry for him, but more than that, I fell in love with him. *We* fell in love," she emphasized. "Neither of us planned on it happening, but…" Her voice trailed off as she relived the few moments they were able to steal away. Looking up again, she continued. "When he told his wife he was filing for a divorce, she went crazy, breaking things, making threats. She

27

threatened to ruin him professionally. When that didn't change his mind, she said she would make sure I never got a job teaching in any school in the country."

Cady frowned. "Nobody has that kind of power. That sounds like something a man would say to get out of a bad situation."

Olivia shook her head. "No, he wouldn't do that. He's an honorable man. He really loved me." Cady didn't argue, but her skeptical look said more than words could.

Olivia's voice got softer as the tale unfolded. She was lost somewhere in the past. "If he didn't love me, he loved you. When I found out I was pregnant, he was ready to give up everything so we could be together. But her threats turned toward you. If Mason had gone through with the divorce, he was afraid that she would harm me and eventually you. He would have died trying to protect us, but I couldn't let that happen either. I knew I had to leave before something happened to all of us." How could she doubt his love after all he'd done for them through the years?

She turned to look at Cady again. "At the time, I wasn't sure if she would carry through with her threats, but Mason believed her. We agreed that to keep our unborn child safe, I would have to go away. His wife said if she ever found out that he had contacted me or you, she would ruin all of us."

"How did she have that kind of power?"

Olivia shrugged. "I'm not sure. But she was able to convince Mason that she was capable of doing what she threatened. Mason is a wealthy man. He bought a failing business from her father when they got married. Under his leadership, it has flourished and expanded to become a name to be recognized all over the country. It now carries his name."

Cady still couldn't remember what his last name was, but it didn't matter. "So how is it that he's able to come here now if she still wields that much power over him? Where are his

28

kids now?"

"His wife recently passed away. You might remember hearing about her death on the news. It was a big deal in some circles. The only thing I know about his older children is what he said when he came here yesterday," Olivia said. "That was the first time I'd seen Mason in more than twenty-one years." There was a wistful note in her voice.

"So he hasn't contacted you in all that time? How did he even know where to find us?"

Olivia sighed. "He's kept track of us. I'm not sure how he kept that from his wife, but he did. She's never tried to harm either of us." Explaining how he had always been a silent part of their lives meant exposing all the lies she'd told over the years. When this was done, would her daughter still love her? It was a risk she had to take. Cady needed to know the truth and she needed to clear her conscience.

When her mother fell silent, Cady rested her head against the back of the couch. It felt like her head was going to explode with all she'd just learned. She vaguely remembered a man congratulating her when she'd graduated. He'd said something about being there for his daughter's graduation. Was that why he'd looked familiar yesterday? Had he popped into her life at other times? She didn't know.

"Wait a minute." She sat up; a frown drew her dark brows together. "You said his wife's death made the news. They have to be pretty famous and wealthy for that to happen." She looked suspiciously at her mom. "What's his last name?"

"Jarvis," Olivia's voice was so soft Cady wasn't sure she heard correctly.

"As in Jarvis House Hotels? The same hotel where Robert is the manager?" The Jarvis name might not be as famous as Hilton and Marriott in the hotel business, but it wasn't far behind. "Did he send Robert here to spy on us, on me? Is that why he asked me out?" She stood up, pacing across the room.

"I'm sure Mason wouldn't do something like that." *Would he?* Olivia silently asked. Remembering what he'd told her about going to some of Cady's soccer games and attending her college graduation, doubts began to creep into her mind. Why would he do that without telling her?

Cady shook her head. "I'll deal with Robert later. Is there anything else you've been keeping from me?"

"Please, Cady, try to understand. We did this to protect you."

"I'm not Snow White and this isn't a fairy tale. The evil queen wasn't going to kill me to retain her power. What would it have hurt either of you to at least tell me who my father was? Did he think I was going to try to claim an inheritance or something?" She flopped down on the couch again only to pop back up. "I'm going for a walk." Before Olivia could try to stop her, she walked out the door.

What's done is done, she told herself. The past can't be changed. What was she going to do with the information she had now? She has a brother and a sister. If what her mom said about them was true, she doubted they had gotten better with time. Did they know about her?

Over the years there had been high-profile cases in the news about wealthy families squabbling over money when a parent dies. Who controlled the family fortune now? Was it Mason or had his late wife left everything to her kids? What would he do if that was the case? She shook her head. It was useless to speculate about that. She knew less than nothing about the Jarvis family fortune.

What she did know was Robert worked for the company Mason ran. Did he know she was Mason's daughter? Is that why he was in Tumbleweed, to spy on her? But who would he be spying for? According to Olivia, Mason knew a lot about her already. He didn't need someone to spy on her. That left Mason's other kids. But they aren't kids now. They are adults.

Spoiled, entitled kids grow up to be spoiled, entitled adults. If they thought she was going to get part of their inheritance, what would they do to her?

It wouldn't hurt to do a little digging into this family she now found herself a part of. As head librarian, she knew how to do research. The internet is an invaluable tool when trying to find information. She might even do a little research on Robert. Other than working for the hotel Mason's family owns, is there another connection?

She'd been walking longer than she'd planned and her feet were beginning to hurt. She was used to walking and hiking through the forest that surrounded the town. But not in a dress and heels, even low heels. She was still wearing Blair's dress as well as the pair of shoes she'd worn to work. As the sun dipped behind the mountain, the temperature was dropping. Even in the summer, the evenings got chilly, especially in the forest. The lightweight dress she was wearing wouldn't keep her warm if she had to spend the night out here.

Stopping to take stock of where she was, she realized she'd gone much further than she planned. Although she'd grown up hiking in these woods, everything looked different after dark. It would be easy to become disoriented and go in the wrong direction. Staying out overnight wasn't something she wanted to do, especially dressed as she was.

It took a moment to orient herself to where she was and which way she needed to go. As she turned, something whizzed past her head. Seconds later she heard the gunshot. "Holy crap," she muttered. Was someone shooting at her? There wasn't time to wonder about that now. Another bullet slammed into the tree next to her sending splinters flying into her face.

CHAPTER FOUR

Crouching down close to the ground to avoid getting shot, made moving difficult. She needed to get out of the woods and around people, but to do that she had to make sure she went in the right direction. Could those shots be heard in town? She had an advantage over the shooter though. She knew these woods like the back of her hand. As long as she kept her head and didn't panic, she would get out of this in one piece.

Pulling her cell phone out of her pocket, she turned it on. Cell reception in the forest was spotty at the best of times. She prayed this wasn't one of the worst of times. Hopefully, whoever was shooting at her wasn't close enough to see the glare from the screen or hear her talking.

When the 911 operator answered, she breathed a sigh of relief. "This is Cady Townsend. I'm in the forest at the edge of town. Someone is shooting at me."

"I'm sorry, Miss. I can't make out what you're saying. You'll need to speak louder."

"I can't. Someone is shooting at me." It was getting darker by the minute. Before long she wouldn't be able to see her hand in front of her face. Listening intently, she didn't hear any movement. Even the night animals were hunkered down after those two shots had been fired.

"Can you tell me where you are?" The operator's calm voice came through her phone.

"I'm in the forest outside of Tumbleweed. Someone has fired two shots at me."

"Can you give me a better location?"

"Oh, let me see, there are pine trees all around me, pine needles on the ground. I'm in the forest. There isn't much description beyond that." Her snarky tone wasn't helping. She paused, taking a calming breath. "I went into the forest from the west off of Third Street and Main." She tried to figure out how long she'd been in the forest."

"All right, Miss, I've reported the shooting. There have been several calls of gunshots in the area. A deputy will be there shortly. Are you injured? Do you need a paramedic?"

"No, I wasn't hit."

"Okay, I'll stay on the line with you until the deputy gets there. Were you able to see who was shooting at you? Are they still shooting?"

The calm voice of the operator helped to calm her already spent nerves. She listened for a moment, realizing there hadn't been any more shots. "No, I guess it's getting too dark for them to see me." When she dropped down, she'd been facing what she thought was the right direction leading to town. Had she gotten turned around? If she moved, would she be going further into the forest instead of out of it?

When the faint sound of a siren could be heard, she cautiously stood up. If she could follow the sound, she would eventually reach civilization. With the police on the way, it would be too risky for the shooter to fire another shot. At least, she hoped that was true. Moving from tree to tree, she stepped as lightly as possible. A branch cracking as she stepped on it would give her location away. Maybe the siren would disguise any noise she made as she moved.

"I hear the police sirens now, so I'm going to hang up." Cady let out a small squeal at the voice in her ear. She'd forgotten the operator was still on the line.

"Are you all right, Miss? Did something happen?"

"No, I'm fine. Thank you." Disconnecting the call, she continued to cautiously move toward the sound of the siren. It felt like it took hours to make her way out of the forest. She hadn't gone as far as she'd thought. Seeing the flashing lights and the floodlight from the top of the big SUV, she stumbled the last few steps out of the trees.

"Are you all right, Miss?" The deputy gripped her arms to keep her from falling. His eyes traveled the length of her, checking for any injuries. There was no blood that he could see, but… *Wow.* His thoughts short-circuited for a second. Her short skirt revealed a pair of fantastic legs. He took a gulping breath in an effort to get his thoughts in check. "I'm Deputy Darrell Flanagan. Do you know who was shooting at you?"

Unable to find her voice, she shook her head. She was just glad to be safe. After hearing shots fired, a crowd had begun to gather at the end of the street. There were several other vehicles parked there as well. Did one of them belong to the shooter? Had he walked out of the forest and now stood watching the action? Another deputy's SUV pulled up to push the crowd back.

She said a small prayer that no one could see her face. She wasn't sure if anyone was using their cell phone to capture what was happening. She didn't want her picture to end up on the front page of the local paper or social media.

Cady looked up at the man as he helped her toward his SUV. His big cowboy hat was pulled low over his forehead and she couldn't make out his features. It didn't matter. He could look like Frankenstein and she would still want to hug him. She was relieved to be safe. He must be new in town or he would recognize her.

"Can you tell me what happened?" he pressed.

"It was getting dark when I realized where I was. If I hadn't turned around…" Realizing what would have happened if she hadn't moved when she did, her breath caught in her throat. "I would be dead," she whispered.

"Are you sure the shots were fired at you? Maybe someone was aiming at an animal. This is the forest." Taking in the way she was dressed, he must have thought she was a tourist and didn't know what she was talking about.

"Yes, I'm sure they were aiming at me. The second shot

only missed because I turned around. I've walked through this forest most of my life. I know what I'm talking about. It isn't even hunting season." Angry at his patronizing tone, she pulled away from him.

"Can you think of anyone who would want to hurt you?"

Her mind swirled with everything her mom had told her tonight. Would Robert shoot at her? He'd acted angry at the thought that she was seeing someone else. His interest in her all along had probably been a lie as well as most everything else in her life. She finally shook her head. "I can't think of anyone who wanted to kill me. I need to go home. My mom will be worried since I've been gone so long. Thank you for coming. I hope I didn't take you away from your family dinner."

"No, Ma'am. No family in town and I'd already eaten." A grin played around his full lips. Standing next to his car, the bright floodlight at his back left his face in shadows. The one feature that stood out was his square chin with a dimple in the center. She was sure he was mocking her. "If you'd like to get in, I'll take you home." He opened the back door for her.

"I can walk. It's not that far." She held her head high and her back was rigid. Someone had taken a shot at her and he was making fun of her. Taking a step away from his vehicle, she groaned. Preoccupied with being shot at, she forgot how much her feet hurt.

Before she could make up her mind, the deputy closed the door. "Okay, if you insist on walking, I'll meet you at your place. What is your address?"

"Why do you need that?" A frown furrowed her forehead.

"I have to fill out a report about shots being fired. This is the forest, but it's still within town limits. It's against the law to fire a gun in the town limits unless for protection. I doubt whoever was firing at you thought you were going to do him harm."

35

She couldn't decide if he was making fun of her again. Just standing there her feet felt like they were ready to fall off. Regardless of what she'd said her house was nearly a mile away. "Oh, all right." She caved. "But do I have to sit in the backseat? I'm not under arrest, am I?" Her heart fluttered at that.

"No, but only law enforcement personnel are allowed in the front seat." He shrugged his broad shoulders. "Department policy."

Her eyes narrowed slightly. Was he telling the truth? With a sigh of resignation, she got in the backseat. Her mom was probably worried since she'd been gone so long. Showing up in the back of a sheriff deputy's car was going to make it even worse.

Within minutes they stopped in front of the house she shared with her mom. She had to wait for him to open the door since the child locks were engaged on the back doors. "Cady, are you all right? What happened?" Olivia ran out of the house before she was out of the backseat. She gathered Cady in her arms, then pulled back to examine her for any injuries the same way the deputy had.

"I'm fine, Mom. Um, this is…" She looked up at the tall deputy. She'd forgotten his name, but the name tag pinned to his shirt said his name was Deputy Flanagan.

"Howdy, Ma'am, I'm Deputy Darrell Flanagan. I brought your daughter home when…"

"When I got lost in the forest," Cady cut him off before he could blurt out what happened. "I just need to talk to the deputy for a few minutes. I'll be in shortly." She hoped her mom would take the hint.

Olivia frowned at her. Cady knew the forest as well as she knew the streets of Tumbleweed. She wouldn't get lost even after dark.

Before anyone could say anything else, a limousine pulled

up behind the deputy's SUV. Cady hung her head, groaning softly. That's just what she needed right now.

"Cady, are you all right?" Mason rushed up to her. If she hadn't held out her hand to stop him, he would have gathered her in for a hug.

"I'm fine. You didn't need to come." She turned her back on him, glaring at her mom. "Please." She gave a small nod toward the house. It was bad enough that the deputy had made fun of her, and her mom was worried, now she had this man to deal with. It was almost too much. Tears of frustration burned at the back of her eyes.

"Mason, let's go inside. Cady will be along in a few minutes." When he hesitated, Olivia tugged at his hand. He reluctantly allowed her to lead him away.

Cady waited until the door was closed behind them before turning back to the deputy. A small gasp escaped her lips as she looked up at him. He'd pushed the big cowboy hat higher on his forehead. For the first time, she could see his face. His startlingly green eyes held a hint of humor. What she could see of his hair in the light from the porch appeared to be red-blonde. His square jaw and high cheekbones set off his handsome face.

"Wow, how can someone so cute be such a jerk?"

When the deputy's eyebrows disappeared into the lock of hair that had fallen across his forehead, Cady slapped her hand over her mouth. "Did I say that out loud?" Her voice was muffled behind her hand.

"Yep, you did."

He didn't appear angry, but she couldn't be sure. Would he arrest her after all? Her face felt like it was on fire. "I'm sorry."

"Sorry you said that, or sorry you said it out loud?" He tipped his head to one side. A teasing grin played around his full lips.

"Both, I guess." She couldn't contain the giggle bubbling up inside her. After being shot at, it felt good to be able to laugh, to simply be alive.

"Can we go sit down on the porch? My feet are killing me." Without waiting for him to answer, she hobbled up the walk. Sinking down in the Adirondack chair with a groan, she kicked off her shoes. "What is it you need to know for your report?" She was finally able to look at him without sticking her foot in her mouth.

"Tell me what happened. Why were you in the forest at this time of night, dressed like you were going to work?"

"I was upset. I needed to take a walk while I mulled over some things. I wasn't paying attention to where I was going. The forest has always been my refuge when I'm upset. I guess I was on auto-pilot." She lifted one shoulder in a shrug.

"All right that explains why you were out there. Who would want to shoot you?"

"I have no idea." Shaking her head, her chin-length blue-black hair fell into her eyes. Giving it an impatient brush away, she looked into the deputy's eyes. They were the deepest green she'd ever seen. For a long moment, they stared at each other lost in their thoughts.

Clearing his throat, Deputy Flanagan stood up. At five feet, eight, Cady wasn't used to having to look up at a man. From her sitting position, she knew he was probably six feet two or three.

"Do you think you could find the same spot again? I'd like to check things out. Maybe the shooter left some evidence behind. It would help if we could find the bullets or some shell casings." When he finally spoke, he startled her out of her reverie. Had he noticed she was staring at him? Of course he did, she told herself while her face grew hot.

"Um, yeah, sure." She'd never been tongue-tied around men before and she didn't like the feeling. "The library is only open from nine until noon tomorrow. My assistant can cover for me until I get there. It won't take long, will it?" A widow in her late fifties, Martha was as reliable as the sun rising in the east and setting in the west. She was working to have something to do since her husband passed on five years ago.

"That isn't necessary. It can wait until you get off work."

Cady shook her head. Waiting until after noon, there would be a bigger chance of being seen. The town busybodies already had enough to talk about after what happened. She didn't want to add to it.

"That's all right. I'd rather get it over with first thing in the morning. I'm sure I can find where I was standing. I hadn't gone too far when the first shot was fired." Talking about what happened made it all too real, and for a minute her head swam.

"Are you okay?" He reached out to touch her arm. Taking several gulping breaths, Cady nodded her head. She wasn't certain that was exactly the truth. But she would be okay.

"What time would you like me to pick you up?"

"Oh, can't I just meet you there? I don't want people seeing me in the back of your car. Everyone will assume I'm under arrest. Besides, I need to go to work when we're finished." After Isabell Brewster's visit to the library earlier, she would pounce on something like this. The woman lived to have something to gossip about.

Darrell nodded. "That's fine. I'll meet you there at...?" One rust-colored eyebrow arched upward as his voice trailed off.

Cady tried to calculate when would be the best time to meet him with the least chance of being seen by everyone in town. She'd always lived within the confines of the law. What would people say about what happened? She wondered how Isabell Brewster would twist this into something salacious. Dismissing that thought, she looked at the deputy. "Is eight o'clock too early? That should give us enough time to find the spot and I can still make it to work by nine."

"I'll see you then." Touching the brim of his hat, he sauntered back to his vehicle.

Tipping her head to one side she watched him walk away. He looked just as good from that vantage point as he did from the front, she decided with a chuckle. She stayed on the porch until the taillights of his big SUV disappeared in the dark.

Knowing her mom was waiting inside for an explanation, she sighed. The talk was going to be awkward enough without having that man there as well. Feeling like she was going to face a firing squad, she picked up her shoes and stood up. She might as well get this over with.

CHAPTER FIVE

Olivia's and Mason's heads were close together when she pushed open the door. A warm blush crept up Olivia's face, and she couldn't quite meet Cady's eyes. What was she supposed to think about that? She already suspected her mom was still in love with him even after all these years. How did she feel about that? She pushed those thoughts aside. She wasn't going to discuss something like that with *him* here.

"Honey, what happened? Are you hurt?" Olivia spoke softly. "Why did a deputy bring you home?" She paused for a moment before going on. "I know you didn't get lost in the forest."

"No, I didn't get lost, but I did end up there," she answered with a sigh. She sank down on the chair facing her mom. She tried not to look at Mason. Her feet still hurt too much to continue standing. "Trying to sort out all the things you told me, I didn't pay attention to where I was going until it started getting dark. I was in the clearing in the woods not far from the edge of town."

Olivia nodded. That was where Cady always went when something was troubling her. "That doesn't explain why a deputy brought you home."

Cady sighed. Telling them that someone shot at her was going to upset Olivia. She had no way of knowing how Mason would take that news. "When I realized where I was, I turned to come back to town. That's when..." She paused, not knowing how much to say. She'd rather not say anything in front of Mason.

"When what?" Mason prompted. "How did that require a deputy?" There was a hard edge to his voice. "I heard there was a report of shots fired somewhere in town." His dark eyes, so like her own, pinned Cady to the chair. Olivia gasped, covering her mouth with her hand.

With another sigh, Cady explained while trying to keep it low key. "Someone was shooting in the forest. I called 911."

"What were they shooting at?" Olivia asked. Her heart was in her throat. "It isn't hunting season and they aren't supposed to be shooting that close to town."

"I didn't see anyone, so I can't answer that question."

"Would you tell us if someone shot at you?" Mason asked softly. Olivia's face got pale, but she didn't say anything when Mason continued. "I know I shouldn't have come here the way I did, but I will do anything to protect you. Maybe the way I handled things before you were born was wrong as well, but I was protecting you and your mom. You might not believe me, but I have loved you all of your life."

"Cady, you have to tell us if someone was shooting at you," Olivia pressed.

"Why would you jump to that conclusion? I don't know anyone who hates me so much they would try to kill me." Her stomach knotted up again. She knew those shots were meant for her, but she didn't want to worry her mom.

"Money is a strong motivator," Mason said. "I'm a very wealthy man. If people thought you were going to get what they think is rightfully theirs, you don't know what they will do."

Olivia turned to him, her eyes large in her white face. "Are you suggesting one of your kids would try to kill Cady because she's your daughter?"

"I don't want to think either of them is capable of something like that but..." He shook his head. "I just don't know. Belinda hated me long before you came into my life. There's no telling what she told Jerrod and Melanie about you."

"Why did your wife hate you? Were you unfaithful with other women besides Mom?"

42

"Cady!"

"No, that's a legitimate question. She has the right to some answers." He patted Olivia's hand. Turning to Cady, he shook his head. "No, the only time I broke my marriage vows was when I fell in love with your mother. Belinda hated me because I took the small company her father had left to flounder and built it into something to be proud of. I changed the name of the company because I didn't want any reminder of what it had been. She couldn't accept that I was successful when her father wasn't."

"What you're saying is one of your kids might have been in the forest trying to shoot me? I don't have any claim on their inheritance."

"Of course you do. You're my daughter."

"I don't want your money," Cady argued. "You can tell them that so they can leave me alone." What kind of monsters had he raised?

Mason collapsed against the back of the couch, staring up at the ceiling. "I don't want to believe either of them would do something like this, but in all honesty, I don't know what either of them is capable of. I'm afraid I haven't always been there for them when they needed someone to protect them from their mother. She managed to turn them against me a long time ago. I'm afraid they aren't very nice people." He sighed at that admission.

"Should I be worried that they're out there stalking me?"

He gave a harsh laugh, shaking his head. "They wouldn't dirty their hands doing anything so base. But they would pay someone to do it for them."

"Speaking of paying someone to do something for you, did you pay Robert to spy on me?" Sparks shot out of dark eyes.

"Robert who?" He seemed perplexed, but was it real?

"Robert Gates, he works for you. Did you send him here to spy on me?

"I don't know anyone by that name, and I certainly wouldn't pay someone to spy on you." He paused. "This was my first visit to the property here," he admitted. "Jerrod wanted to prove himself to me and asked to have a property that he could take through construction to managing it. From the looks of the hotel, he didn't follow the guidelines used on every other hotel in the chain." *One more slap in the face by one of his kids,* he thought. "You said he works for me? In what capacity?"

"He's the manager of your hotel right here in Tumbleweed."

When Olivia would have said something to Cady about her tone, Mason laid his hand on her arm. "Whatever she's feeling about me right now, I deserve." His dark eyes turned back to Cady. "The manager of this hotel is Robert Gaston, not Robert Gates. I haven't had the opportunity to speak with him. Since I'm not here on business I didn't feel it was necessary." He was getting a bad feeling about this.

Cady stared at him, trying to tell if he was lying. She'd never had a reason to go to the hotel, before or after she met Robert. They always met somewhere for lunch, or he picked her up at home. The restaurant in the hotel was more upscale than other restaurants in town, and he'd never taken her there. Was that because he didn't want her to know his real name, or because he didn't work at the hotel as he said?

"Would your son hire someone to spy on me, maybe take potshots at me to scare me off?" Robert hadn't been all that interested in going into the forest. It would surprise her if he'd been the shooter. But she could see him spying on her. Even his appearance at the library that morning was suspect now.

"These are questions I'll be asking both Mr. Gaston and Jerrod. He is even the one that advocated having a hotel built here in Tumbleweed."

"Did you know this is where Mom and I live? Did he

know?"

"Of course, I knew. In hindsight, I suppose Jerrod knew as well. If Belinda knew, both Jerrod and Melanie knew. I wasn't in favor of building the hotel here. It was too tempting to have one so close to the two of you since I travel between the properties making sure things are being run properly. But Jerrod had been asking to have a site all of his own. I was hoping it was a sign that he was finally going to take an interest in the business and not just the money it produces." He sighed wearily. "I should have known better."

"If Jerrod knows Robert, would he have him spying on us?" Olivia asked.

"That's a question I'll be asking Mr. Gaston first thing in the morning. I'll also be asking him where he was tonight while someone was shooting at you." If Jerrod was behind this attempt on Cady's life, he would make sure his son paid for it. He'd missed the first twenty-one years of his daughter's life. He wasn't going to have her taken away from him now.

~~~

His arrival at the hotel had caused quite a stir among the staff on duty the night before. The young woman at the front desk wanted to call the manager, but he'd told her not to bother. He wasn't there on business. His mind had been consumed with the way he'd handled things with Cady. It had been a big mistake coming here the way he had. It was a mistake he hoped he'd be able to overcome.

Although each of his properties had a similar image, they were all upscale. As a boy, he'd enjoyed staying at several bed and breakfasts with his parents. They always gave the feeling of being at home. Each one was like a luxury home instead of a hotel. He'd wanted to build something like that. He'd wanted something that stood out from other hotel chains. Each site was owned by Mason Jarvis, Inc. It wasn't a publicly-traded company.

Mason was a hands-on type of person. When a new property was being developed, he was there right from the start of the project. This was supposed to be Jerrod's chance to prove what he could do, so Mason had stayed away. He'd trusted Jerrod to make the right decisions. Apparently, that trust had been misplaced.

Although he couldn't complain about the hotel itself, it was no different from so many other hotels in any other chain. It didn't resemble the other hotels in his chain. Was that Jerrod's way of giving his father the finger? He shook his head. He'd deal with Jerrod later.

He'd spent his first night and the next day worrying about Cady. He'd been tempted to go to the library to see her. But trying to see her while she was at work would have been another mistake. He'd made enough of those concerning her. He didn't need to make any more.

When he was inspecting a property, he never announced his arrival beforehand. Prior knowledge of his visit defeated the purpose of an inspection. Once a manager knew he was there, they bent over backward to make sure he found everything was as he wanted.

This was his first visit to the Tumbleweed property. He'd been surprised that the manager hadn't come to his room that morning once he'd learned the company owner and CEO was on the premises.

When Olivia had called that Cady had walked out after their talk, he'd wanted to be with her. But again he thought that would be a mistake. Cady needed time to take in everything her mother had told her. Forcing himself on her at this point wasn't going to help matters.

Cady had been gone over an hour when Olivia called a second time. Her voice had been filled with worry. When he heard about shots fired somewhere in town, he went straight to Olivia's. Pulling up behind the sheriff deputy's vehicle at

Olivia's home nearly stopped his heart. If something had happened to Cady, he would never forgive himself. He'd allowed Belinda's threats to keep him from knowing his daughter.

His first priority the next morning was to have a discussion with Robert Gaston. Had Jerrod sent him here to spy on Olivia and Cady? Had he tried to shoot Cady? One way or another, he was going to get to the bottom of this. Both Jerrod and Robert Gaston were about to find out who the boss of this operation was.

The fact that Robert Gaston still hadn't come to his room confirmed his suspicion that Robert Gaston and Robert Gates were one and the same. It was time for the mountain to go to Mohamad.

"Hello, Mr. Gaston." Mason knocked on the manager's door, pushing it open without waiting to be invited in. "Or should I call you Mr. Gates?" He leaned casually against the threshold, crossing one leg over the other at the ankle. He was good at concealing the tension and anger bubbling up inside him. The room was much bigger than any offices in his other hotels. That was probably because Jerrod envisioned himself sitting behind that desk someday. But if that was the case, why was Robert here instead of Jerrod? He pushed that aside. He had more important matters to discuss.

"Hello, Mr. Jarvis." Robert stood up. "Please come in and have a seat. I heard that you were in town, but I was told you weren't here on business." His forehead creased slightly in a frown of confusion. "Why did you call me Mr. Gates? As you must be aware, my name is Robert Gaston."

"That's right. That's what it says on your personnel records. But Cady said your name is Robert Gates. You can imagine my confusion at that. Maybe you'd like to explain why you would use a different name when you introduced yourself to her." He walked across the room, taking a seat in one of the plush chairs in front of the desk.

"I'm sorry, Sir, I don't know what you're talking about. I would never use a false name. She must have misunderstood me. Gaston and Gates are very similar. I'm not sure what business it is of yours anyway."

"Is that really how we're going to play this game?" Mason waited to see what the other man would say. When he remained silent, Mason continued. "I'm sure you're aware that Cady is my daughter, Jerrod's half-sister."

"Your daughter? No Sir, I wasn't aware of that. Jerrod never said anything about having a half-sister. If I'd known that, I might not have approached her. Dating the boss's sister, half or otherwise, isn't a good business decision."

Oh, he's smooth all right, Mason thought. "Ultimately, Jerrod isn't your boss. I am. Where were you last night between six-thirty and seven o'clock?"

"What business is that of yours? What I do in my spare time has no bearing on my job." Robert leaned back in the big chair, resting his hands across his flat stomach. This wasn't going the way he'd planned.

"It's my business because someone tried to kill my daughter."

Robert sat up straight, giving a small gasp. "That's horrible. Is she all right?" As though realizing the implication of Mason's question, he frowned. "Are you suggesting I tried to kill her? I think you need to leave. Now." He stood up so fast his chair slammed against the wall.

Mason remained seated. "You really think you can throw your boss out of your office? That isn't going to happen. I'll give you sixty minutes to collect your personal belongings and vacate this office. You're fired."

"You can't fire me." Robert sat down again, a smug smile on his lips.

"And why is that?" One dark eyebrow arched upward.

"Because you don't own this hotel."

"Is that right? Then who, pray tell, does own it?"

"Me and my family." Robert acted like he held all the cards in whatever game he was playing.

"Who is your family?"

Robert chuckled. "I'm not surprised you don't know. You never were interested in your wife's family. You'll have to be interested now, because Jerrod is helping me reclaim what rightfully belongs to my family, starting with this hotel. He signed everything concerning the hotel over to me. We're going to rid you of your hotel empire. When we're finished, you won't have a pot to pee in or a window to throw it out of."

Anger burned Mason's stomach. He never realized how much his son hated him. "That sounds like something Belinda's kin would say," he stated mildly. "I'm not sure she would express things in quite those terms though. How, exactly, are you related to Belinda?" As any good businessman in a tight situation, his face revealed nothing of what was going on inside him.

"She and my mother were sisters. Their father started this company long before you hijacked it."

Mason chuckled. "I guess your grandfather didn't tell anyone that he gave me the company as a wedding present when I married your aunt. Why do you think Belinda hated him and consequently me? I made a success out of something he'd never been able to do."

For a long moment, Robert appeared confused. When he stood up again, there was a grim look on his face. "I have all the paperwork showing how you cheated my grandpa out of his business. If you're prepared for a long drawn-out court battle..." He shrugged. "So be it. I'll see you in court. Now please leave my office, or I'll be forced to call the sheriff's department and have you removed."

"Go ahead and call them, but it won't be me leaving this

office. My name is still on this hotel and all the paperwork concerning it. I still pay the bills around here. If you think I'm going to turn anything of mine over to you, you're wrong. I doubt that you can run this place without my money backing you. I'll stop paying your salary and that of everyone working here. How loyal will your staff be then? I'll stop paying for water, electricity, and everything else I've paid for. In case you aren't aware, that comes to a pretty big chunk of change every month.

"As far as a court battle goes, I have the resources to fight you all the way. I have every piece of paper your grandpa signed proving this and every other hotel in the Jarvis line is mine. Your grandfather had two small motels that I turned into a mega-company. Do you think that he would have been able to build what I have today?"

He waited for Robert to say something. When he remained silent, he continued. "Although he said the company was a wedding present, I paid him far more than those motels were worth. He has no claim on anything I turned them into. And neither do you." He stood up, looking at the younger man. "You have one hour to vacate this office. A member of security will be with you while you clean out your desk to ensure you take only your personal items. If you insist on making a scene, the sheriff's department will be called in. My attorneys will be in touch."

Turning to leave, he stopped at the door looking back at Robert. "If I find out that you are the one that shot at Cady last night, you won't have to worry about attorneys." There was a quiet threat in his voice.

Robert sat down, trying to slow the rapid beating of his heart. He'd expected there would be a confrontation eventually, but this went beyond what he'd been expecting. He'd heard all the stories about how his grandpa had been building a major hotel chain when Mason Jarvis stole the company right out from under him. But how much of it was true?

By the time Robert was born, the old geezer did little more than sit around drinking and cursing Mason Jarvis and the loss of his company. Belinda had promised she would help him take back what should have belonged to his mother's family. But she was dead. What would Jerrod do? He hadn't been aware of their relationship until recently. Would Jerrod side with him or his father?

Robert shook his head. He seriously doubted Jerrod would help him in any way. He'd already been complaining about Robert taking over what should have been his. He'd folded at the first sign of his mother backing Robert instead of him. The guy had about as much starch in his backbone as wet spaghetti. He only stuck to something that was solid and could hold him up. That would be his old man, not Robert.

CHAPTER SIX

What has Jerrod done this time? Mason paced around the large suite. Should he call Jerrod now or wait until he got back to San Francisco? He shook his head. Waiting wasn't an option. Someone had tried to kill Cady. Besides, he planned on spending as much time in Tumbleweed as Olivia and Cady would allow. He wasn't going anywhere. He picked up his phone. Of course, Jerrod denied knowing anything about what was going on here. How much of what he said could he believe?

His attorney would deal with Robert Gaston. No one was going to run him out of his own hotel. Would Gaston be bold enough and foolish enough to use a master key card to gain entry into his room? After the conversation with the man, he wouldn't put anything past him. But staying somewhere else was akin to admitting defeat. He wasn't about to do that.

He wasn't here to wrangle with Robert Gaston or Belinda's deadbeat old man. Mason knew the man was alive. Belinda had been sending him money every month since the day she and Mason were married. She'd said it was the least she could do since Mason had taken away his livelihood.

Running his long fingers through his hair, he sank down onto the armchair only to bounce back up. He couldn't sit around while someone had tried to kill Cady. He had to protect her. Would she even accept his help?

He would protect all of his children with the same vigor. But the only thing Jerrod and Melanie wanted from him was his money. Melanie was a drunk like her mother. She'd gotten so many tickets for DUI that her license had been revoked. It was only by the grace of God that she hadn't killed herself or someone else. To keep that from happening, he'd hired a chauffeur. It hadn't stopped her drinking, but at least no one else was going to die because of her.

Jerrod only drank occasionally, but he certainly wasn't an upstanding citizen. The fact that he had probably helped Robert with this little con game was proof of that. Jerrod was more concerned with his own bottom line than anything else. If he thought Cady was going to get one cent of what he considered his, he would do anything to stop that from happening. Did that include murder?

Jerrod had seemed upset when he learned what Robert was saying, but again was it all part of their game? How much of what Jerrod said could he trust to be the truth?

Belinda had still been alive when Jerrod campaigned for this hotel to be built. Had she been behind that? Had she planned on Robert taking over instead of Jerrod? Is that how Robert was placed as the manager? Was Jerrod aware that Robert was his cousin? Of course, he was, he answered the question himself. Why else would he sign over this hotel to him? He had too many questions and not enough answers.

Jerrod and Melanie had been nothing more to Belinda than pawns in her game against Mason. He had tried for years to protect them from the hatred she spewed until he finally gave up. She had bought them off and turned them against him. There was nothing he could do. Even from beyond the grave, Belinda was pulling strings and reaching out to touch everything he'd ever held dear.

His job now was to protect Olivia and Cady. He needed to find out who had tried to kill her. What was the sheriff's department doing to find the person?

Taking his laptop and anything else that had personal information attached to it, Mason walked out of the suite. He wasn't going to let that pipsqueak Robert run him out of his own hotel. But he wouldn't leave behind anything that might benefit the man either. There were ways to prevent even the manager's master key card from accessing the room.

Once in the limo, he placed a call to his attorney. Matthew Connelly was as savvy as any lawyer he knew. Mason wasn't worried about losing even one of his hotels to Belinda's family, but he needed to give Matthew a heads up about what might be on the horizon.

~~~

Cady left her car in the parking lot at the trailhead leading into the forest. She was surprised to see Deputy Flanagan's county-issued SUV already waiting for her. She checked her watch to see if she was late. *No, he's early,* she thought. She liked that in a man. He didn't expect others to sit around waiting for him.

As she walked up to his vehicle, he stepped out. Again she was struck by the fact that he towered over her by five or more inches. There were few men who bested her by that much. She liked that as well. A smile lifted the corners of her mouth.

"Good morning, Miss Townsend. How are you this morning?" He touched the brim of his cowboy hat in greeting.

"I'm fine. And please call me Cady."

"All right, Cady." A crooked smile tilted his lips upward revealing a small dimple in one cheek. His bright green eyes sparkled with mischief.

She wondered what that was all about. Was he here to humor her? Didn't he believe someone had shot at her? A frown creased her forehead. If he didn't believe her, this was a waste of time. Even if they found the bullet or a shell casing, that would only prove that someone had been shooting, not necessarily at her.

This morning she was dressed more sensibly for a hike in the woods with jeans, a long-sleeved shirt, and hiking boots. She had a change of clothes in the car. When they finished here, she still needed to go to work. "Shall we get started? I think I can lead you close to where I was when those shots were fired." She turned away from those piercing eyes.

For several minutes neither of them spoke. When the silence began to get awkward, she cleared her throat. "Something came to me in the middle of the night." She refused to look up at him. She didn't want to know if he was laughing at her.

He seemed to be waiting for her to continue. Sighing, she finished her thought. "Whoever shot at me was using a handgun, not a rifle."

"Why do you say that?" He finally spoke up.

"I know the difference between the sound of a rifle and a handgun." When he appeared skeptical, she bristled. "I've lived next to the forest my entire life. I've even gone hunting once or twice. I've been target practicing since before I was in high school. I own a gun, all perfectly legal," she added, "and I'm a pretty good shot." She didn't know if she was trying to impress him with her shooting ability or the fact that she knew the difference between the sound of a handgun and a rifle.

Tilting her head to look up at him, her stomach fluttered. Why was he always smiling at her? Was he mocking her? She felt off-balance every time she looked at him. When he simply nodded without saying anything, she decided it was best if she kept any further thoughts to herself.

As the silence stretched out, her nerves were stretched taut. Something about this man set her nerves on edge. She breathed a sigh of relief when she stopped at the edge of a small clearing. "This is where I was last night." She pointed out the scuffed marks on the ground where she had been standing when the first shot was fired. The imprint of the low-heeled shoes she'd been wearing the night before was still visible in the dirt.

"Do you believe me now?"

"I never said I didn't believe you." He shook his head.

"Actions speak louder than words," she snapped. "You've been making fun of me ever since we met."

He shook his head. "I never meant to make you feel like that. It just seemed a little implausible that someone was shooting this close to town. Considering how you were dressed, I thought you were a tourist and had wandered into the woods by mistake and got scared."

"Tourists don't usually wear dresses when they're on vacation. Besides, what does the way I was dressed have to do with someone shooting at me? You thought I was making that part up." It was an accusation. He had the grace to look embarrassed by that fact. "The second shot hit the tree I was standing close to. If I hadn't crouched down, I would have been hit and this conversation would have taken a different turn. If it happened at all," she added.

"Yes, and I'm sorry. You didn't mention the last shot hit the tree. I might be able to find the bullet."

"Forgive me for being a little rattled," she said sarcastically. "It isn't every day that someone shoots at me."

Ignoring her sarcasm, he stepped further into the clearing. There were a lot of trees surrounding the small area. "Can you tell me approximately where you were standing? Do you know which tree was hit?" He looked over his shoulder at her.

For a minute she replayed those few seconds when she realized she was no longer in town before the shots were fired. They had felt like an eternity. There were a lot of scuff marks in the dirt and the pine needles were brushed aside in several places. Being careful not to erase her footprints from the night before, she stepped into the clearing. "When I realized how far I'd walked, I turned back the way I came. That's when I felt something fly past me. Seconds later I heard the retort from the gun. As I crouched down, the second bullet hit the tree." She looked around. The trees all looked alike.

"I think I was standing right about here." She looked down at the scuff marks in the dirt. "It would have to be one of these trees." She pointed at three trees standing close together.

Methodically examining each tree, it only took a minute to find where the first bullet grazed the tree. The second bullet was embedded in the bark just below where the first bullet struck. Taking a rather large knife out of the top of his boot, he proceeded to dig the bullet out of the tree. He was careful not to add any additional marks on the metal.

As the bullet fell into the small plastic evidence bag, Cady's head began to swim. Seeing the bullet drove home the fact that if she hadn't turned when she did, she could be dead. A guardian angel had been with her the night before.

Looking around, Darrell gauged the approximate direction the shot came from. Lost in his thoughts, he took off. Unwilling to be left behind, Cady followed him. She wanted to know where he was going. They hadn't gone far when he stopped and turned in the direction they'd come.

He shook his head. "It's a pretty clear line of sight from here to where you were standing. It was dumb luck that he missed you."

"There is no such thing as luck. I prefer to call it a blessing that he missed." A chill moved through her. Whoever shot at her had been standing less than fifty feet from where she'd been.

"Do you recall hearing any movement before the shot?"

She shook her head. "No. I had a lot on my mind."

"What were you doing out here dressed as though you had just gotten off work?"

She sighed. "I *had* just gotten off work." How much of what was going on in her personal life did she need to tell him? Would it help find the shooter to layout their dirty laundry for everyone to see? "My mom and I had a disturbing conversation. I needed time to sort through my feelings so I went for a walk." She shrugged. "I wasn't planning on walking that far. Being in the forest has always been my source of refuge when I'm upset."

"What was this disturbing conversation about?"

"Does that matter?" A frown drew her dark brows together as she looked up at him. The sunlight filtering through the trees made it hard to see his features already shaded by the brim of his big cowboy hat. She didn't want to air her family's dirty laundry to a stranger.

"You never know what matters in a crime." He waited patiently for her to answer.

"I had just met my..." She hesitated. What was she supposed to call Mason Jarvis? *Certainly not Dad,* she decided. "I had just met my biological father the night before," she finally finished her statement.

"That's the man in the limo?" One rust-colored eyebrow arched up.

Sighing, she nodded. "Thursday was my birthday and he came here to meet me."

"Wow. That must have been a birthday surprise to top all surprises."

Nodding her head, her dark hair swung around her face. "I had come home from work to talk to my mom about that. I was understandably upset. I needed time to sort through my feelings." There were still a lot of things she needed to sort through. She didn't want to talk about Mason. "What's the next step?" But Darrell had more questions.

"Do you know where he's staying? Since that's the first limousine I've seen in Tumbleweed, I take it he's not from around here. Do you know where he lives?"

Cady shrugged. "I have no idea where he lives. As I said, I had just met him. I'm guessing he's staying at the Jarvis House Hotel since he owns it." She watched Darrell's face for his reaction to her comment. When he remained stone-faced, she decided he would be a heck of a poker player.

Without making any comment, he started searching the ground moving out in a wider radius. Stooping down, he retrieved a shell casing. Taking a pen from his pocket, he picked it up and slid it into another evidence bag. "Maybe we'll get lucky, um, blessed," he winked at her, "and there will be a partial print on this." Widening his search further, he came up with the second shell casing. He did the same thing with that one as he had the first. It had been too dark the night before for the shooter to police his brass. That had been in their favor.

"I think that's all we're going to find here. You ready to head back?"

Cady looked around. She wished there was something to tell her who wanted her dead. Mason had a son and daughter. He said they weren't very nice people. But were they capable of hiring someone to kill her? Her thoughts were jumbled as she led the way out of the forest.

"Thank you for meeting me this morning," Darrell said when they stopped beside his SUV. When a gust of wind blew her dark hair into her face, she gave it an impatient push. The silky strands caused his fingers to itch with the desire to push it away for her. "What else can you tell me about your... ah..." She hadn't called him her dad. That left the field open for a lot of descriptions. Was she adopted? That could explain why she just met him.

"My birth father," she filled in the blank, arching a dark brow at him. "As you might have guessed, I don't know much about him. Until two nights ago I thought he was dead."

That got a reaction from him as a frown creased his forehead, but he patiently waited for her to continue. When she didn't, he prompted her. "And?"

"And nothing." She shrugged. "Since my mother never said anything about him, I assumed he was dead."

"You never asked?"

She sighed. "No, and that was my mistake. He never came up in conversation. Maybe most kids would have asked about their dad, but I didn't. I wasn't curious about him. My life was full of people who loved me. I wasn't the only kid growing up without a father. I never felt like I was missing something." Questions beat at his mind, but the answers had nothing to do with the case. He wanted to know about Cady for his own reasons. "What is his name? You said he owns Jarvis House Hotels?" It was a question.

"Yes, his name is Mason Jarvis. I have no idea where he lives. I'm assuming he's staying at his hotel here in town, but you'll have to verify that yourself."

"You've had some time to think about what happened. Have you thought of someone who would want to harm you? Is there anyone you've recently had problems with? A boyfriend, a co-worker, anyone?" He watched her expressive face as her emotions played out. He would love to know what she was thinking.

Robert had put on a show of being upset at the thought of her seeing someone else. But she was certain that's all it had been, a show. She'd never considered him anything other than a friend and had been under the impression he felt the same. After learning who Mason Jarvis was, she was convinced that Robert had been spying on her. But for whom? Would he have a reason to want to hurt her?

Should she tell Darrell about Mr. Jarvis' son and daughter? She couldn't even remember their names. They were probably good suspects, but she wasn't going to throw them under the bus until she knew for sure they were behind the shooting.

"You've thought of someone," he said. "Who?"

She shook her head. "I don't know why anyone would want to hurt me. I'm a librarian in a small town. I don't have anything someone else would want."

He still thought she was holding back. He wanted to know what. Why would she withhold information if someone wanted her dead? Why wouldn't she tell him? Did she suspect who had shot at her? Who was she protecting? He'd let it go for now, but he'd come back to it later.

"Okay, what about Mason Jarvis? He's your birth father. Why are you just meeting him? Were you adopted?"

A dark frown drew her brows together. He was getting too personal. "No. What does that have to do with someone shooting at me?"

"Jarvis is very wealthy since he owns one of the premier hotel chains in the country. Does he have other children? If so, someone might be afraid you are going to take their inheritance."

Cady sighed. He was going to keep digging. "Yes, he has a son and daughter. They're older than me. And no, I've never met them," she added before he could ask.

"Do they know about you?"

She shrugged. "Yes, I believe they know about me."

"Will you tell me their names?"

She was silent for so long he thought she wasn't going to answer him. She finally shrugged, shaking her head. "I know he told me their names last night, but with everything else I've learned in the last forty-eight hours, I can't remember what he said. Sorry."

"That's all right. I'll get that information from Mr. Jarvis."

"Is that necessary? You don't need to talk to him about this. Besides, I don't want him to think I'm accusing his kids of doing this."

"You're one of his kids," he reminded her. "And yes, it's necessary. Someone either tried to kill you or scare you away. I want to find out who that someone is." That came out sounding a little too personal and he quickly added, "It's my job to find out."

Cady sighed. There was nothing she could do to stop him. Besides, she'd rather find out now before they tried something else. She didn't want to end up in the hospital or worse, the

61

morgue. "Fine. Just don't tell him I accused them of doing this."

"If he cares anything about you, I'm sure he'll want to catch whoever did this." He paused for a moment. "Care to share who else you were thinking about a few minutes ago?"

"Again with that? I don't have a boyfriend and I don't have that type of girlfriend. Any rivals I had in school have either left town or grown up enough not to want me dead."

"But you had thought of someone," he pressed.

"Okay." The word came out on a sigh. "I was supposed to go to dinner with a friend two nights ago. At least I thought he was a friend," she qualified. "That's when Mr. Jarvis showed up. I was so upset I forgot about our dinner arrangements until later. When I did remember, I called him to cancel. He was sitting outside my house. The limo was there." She shrugged. "He accused me of having a better offer, as he called it, and was upset. Or he pretended to be upset."

"Why do you say he pretended to be upset?" A frown drew his brows together.

"He's the manager at Mr. Jarvis' hotel. I think someone had been paying him to spy on me. That is speculation on my part though. Mr. Jarvis said he was going to talk with him."

"I think I'll talk with him as well. What's his name?"

"Robert Gates, I mean Robert Gaston. He even gave me a phony name when I met him." She couldn't believe how naïve she'd been about this and so many other things in her life.

Taking a card out of the pocket of his western-cut uniform shirt, he handed it to her. "If you think of anything else or something else happens, give me a call. My cell number is on there as well."

He reluctantly watched her walk away. Tumbleweed is a small town. They couldn't help but bump into each other again. Hopefully next time, it wouldn't involve someone shooting at her.

CHAPTER SEVEN

Cady finally made it to the library shortly before it was to open. As she pulled into her parking spot an old man stepped out from behind the dumpster. For an instant, she thought her heart was going to jump out of her chest. When recognition caught up with her brain, she released the breath she'd been holding.

The man waited for her to step out of her car before coming closer. "Morning, Miss Cady." A worried frown creased his forehead. "News is all over town about what happened to you last night. Are you okay?"

"Good morning, Henry. I'm fine. A little shook up is all." Henry was one of the few homeless people in Tumbleweed. He'd made a cozy niche for himself behind the dumpster. When he first showed up, Cady worried he would freeze to death once the really cold weather hit, but he seemed content staying there.

"Don't know why anyone would want to hurt a nice young lady like you," he groused. "Them state troopers working to find the culprit?"

"Yes, they are. I forgot to bring you something this morning. I'm sorry." She had taken to stopping at the donut shop for a couple of donuts and a cup of coffee for him as she came to work. She thought it was the least she could do. This morning she had other matters on her mind.

"Don't you worry about that, Miss Cady. I got myself a secret stash of food in my hidey-hole. I'm not gonna starve. You have a good day." He picked up the broom leaning against the wall. "It's time for me to go to work too." A cackling laugh escaped his lips revealing his toothless gums.

He swept the parking lots of several stores each morning including the front parking lot at the library. For that, the businesses gave him something to eat and drink or maybe a few dollars to spend on something else. She hoped he didn't use it on drugs or alcohol.

Dismissing Henry, she hurried inside. Her assistant would have everything ready to start the day, but she hated being late. Her mom's motto was it's better to be early than late. She tried to live up to that, but sometimes it wasn't easy. Today was one of those days.

~~~

School was almost out for the summer, and Olivia would be grateful for the break. As much as she enjoyed teaching, her life had suddenly gotten very complicated. She didn't know what Mason's intentions were toward her and Cady. Cady was his daughter and she knew he would do his best to keep her safe after what happened the other night.

She wished he had prepared her for his visit instead of simply showing up. What would she have said if he asked first? She wasn't certain what her answer would have been. If there was such a thing as love at first sight, that's what had happened to her all those years ago. After she found out she was pregnant with Cady, she'd had little choice but to leave. Belinda was crazy with her hatred. She'd feared for her life and that of her unborn baby.

If the woman was still alive, Olivia would say she was behind the shooting. But she was gone. Was someone else doing her bidding from the grave? That was crazy. She knew Belinda was capable of almost anything, but reaching up from the grave to get her revenge wasn't one of them.

Tumbleweed is a small town. People were already speculating about the owner of Jarvis House Hotels showing up in their small town and what his appearance at her house meant. Add someone shooting at Cady, and the busybodies' tongues were wagging.

Several teachers had asked her about Mason's presence at

her house. But it wasn't the teachers she was concerned with. Isabell Brewster was the head of the Ladies Book Club, but she was also the biggest gossip in Tumbleweed. She never let anything get past her. If the story wasn't juicy enough, she was known to embellish the truth to fit her narrative. She didn't care who got hurt in the telling either. She'd already been questioning Cady about the limo. By now, Isabell would know it belonged to Mason.

Few people were brave enough to stand up to Isabell. They preferred hunkering down until the talk passed by. What would Mason do if Isabell started spreading a bunch of lies about him or Cady? He wasn't the sort to stand by while someone he cared about was being trashed. Olivia sighed. How had her quiet life turned upside down almost overnight?

~~~

"I heard about what happened last night." When their schedules allowed, Blair and Cady met for lunch every Saturday at The Crossroads Diner in town. "Are you okay? Did you see who was shooting at you?"

Before Cady could do more than shake her head, Isabell Brewster stopped beside their booth. "I heard about what happened to you last night." She didn't bother with a greeting. "I can't believe someone would actually try to kill one of our upstanding citizens right here in town." She sounded sincere when she was really on the prowl for gossip.

"Does that mean it's okay to try killing them somewhere else?" Blair asked mildly. Her eyebrows arched up.

"Of course not." Isabell glared at her for a second before turning back to Cady. "I hope that deputy I saw you with this morning finds this person before more of our citizens become a target."

"Yes, Ma'am, I'm sure he's doing everything possible to find the person."

"Were you able to find what you were looking for in the

65

forest?" She wasn't going to be put off.

Cady shrugged. "That's something you'll have to ask the deputy. He didn't share his findings with me."

When that topic didn't net anything interesting, Isabell tried a different one. "I had assumed Robert had rented that limo to take you out for your birthday, but it seems someone even bigger is in town?" Her eyes were now alight with the idea of finding a juicy tidbit to share with her followers.

"I'm sorry you were wrong in your assumption, but we all know what assuming anything does."

Isabell frowned in confusion. "No, I don't." When Blair giggled, she shot another glare in her direction before quickly turned back to Cady. "It seems the owner of Jarvis House Hotels came to pay a visit to your mother. I wasn't aware she knew someone so important. She never said."

Cady shrugged. "I guess she didn't think her acquaintance with him was anyone else's business."

"It's been nice talking to you, Isabell," Blair interrupted, looking over the woman's shoulder at the waitress standing there. "We're ready to order, Alice." Isabell glared at each of them before flouncing away.

Alice shook her head. "That woman is in here every day hoping to pick up some gossip. When she can't find any here, she heads straight for Clip and Snip. Most folks know not to say anything they want to be kept confidential when she's around. I've even heard she'd tried bugging several places so she knows exactly what's being said at any given time."

"That's our clue not to say anything either," Cady said. "I think I'll have the Southwestern Grilled Cheese sandwich with fries." As much as she wanted to tell her best friend the latest news, she wasn't going to say anything. Several others from the Ladies Book Club had just come into the diner. Isabell had probably called in reinforcements when she couldn't get the information she wanted.

"Is there any place private in this town?" Blair wondered out loud. "I didn't think Isabell was so desperate for gossip that she was willing to send out spies or bug businesses."

Cady shrugged. "I guess we'll have to find something safe to talk about until we leave here."

"Right you are." Blair leaned across the table, keeping her voice down. "Do you remember when we were in high school and we did crazy things just to see how fast she started rumors?"

Cady giggled, nodding her head. "I also remember the night we saw her and her husband leaving their neighbor's house. They didn't know we were sitting in the dark car parked at the curb." Both girls started giggling.

"I thought she was going to squash her poor husband when she jumped on his back for a piggy-back ride home."

"I wonder if those dear ladies know about that night." Cady nodded her head at the women sitting in the booth close to them.

"You think we should inform them?"

"Nah, I'm not willing to stoop to her level. It was enough to see her reaction the next morning when I asked her about her ride home the night before." They were still giggling when Alice set their food on the table. Talk ceased while they concentrated on the food.

"All right, tell me what's going on. Who was shooting at you?" Blair asked when they were safely inside Cady's car where no one could eavesdrop. "What is that deputy doing to find out who shot at you?"

"I'm not sure how much can be done." She pushed her hair behind her ear. "He found the shell casings and the bullet embedded in the tree. But unless the gun has been used in another crime those aren't going to lead anywhere. Darrell…"

"Darrell?" Blair interrupted. Her eyebrows shot up, almost reaching her hairline. A teasing grin played around her mouth.

"Okay, Deputy Flanagan, is that better?"

"No, I like Darrell, but we digress. Tell me what your mom said." She held up her hand before Cady could say anything. "You don't have to tell me anything if you don't want to talk about... him."

"Him who?" Cady teased back. "Are you asking about Mason Jarvis or Deputy Darrell?"

"Mason *Jarvis*," Blair gasped. "As in Jarvis House Hotels? Is he your dad?" Unable to keep the shock out of her voice, she whispered as though someone might be eavesdropping on their conversation.

"Apparently so," Cady said with a sigh. "It turns out Mom is pretty good at keeping secrets. She never said anything when they started building that hotel." She got quiet for a moment. "I guess that accounted for why she was upset when the town first heard about the new hotel going up. She was probably afraid of what was going to happen once it opened."

"Why didn't she ever say anything? Why wait twenty-one years to spring it on you?"

"From the story they told me last night, they were both afraid of what his wife was going to do if the truth came out. She died last month."

"Wife. Oh, boy." Blair gave a soft whistle.

"Yeah," Cady sighed. "I was born on the wrong side of the blanket, as they said in the olden days. I'm not sure what's going to happen now."

"But why would someone try to kill you now if his wife is dead?" Blair frowned. "Did she die under suspicious circumstances?"

Cady gaped at her friend. "I have no idea. You don't suppose..." Her voice trailed off. She didn't want to think the woman had been murdered. "I vaguely remember the news item on TV. I don't remember them saying anything about the cause of death at the time. But if it was suspicious, wouldn't there be something more on the news?"

"Yeah, I guess so." For several minutes, they sat there contemplating that possibility. "What are you going to do? What did Mr. Jarvis have to say?"

Cady preferred thinking of him as Mr. Jarvis as opposed to her birth father. When she finished relaying all that she could remember of her conversation with her mom and *him*, she leaned back on the couch. They had made their way to Blair's apartment while they were talking.

"Have you talked to Robert since that night?"

Cady sniffed. "He was waiting for me when I got to the library the next morning. I still didn't know Mr. Jarvis' last name at the time. Learning that has put a whole different spin on Robert's presence in Tumbleweed. He's probably been spying on me for someone. I'm just not sure who that is. Mr. Jarvis went to talk to him this morning."

She gave a little chuckle. "I'm sure that was an interesting conversation. He was pretty angry when he found out Robert had used a fake name when I met him." A warm blush crept up her neck. "I actually accused him of hiring Robert to spy on me." She gave a soft chuckle. "He said he'd never met Robert." She shrugged. "Considering all the other lies I've heard in my life that could be another one. It turns out I'm not very good at telling when someone is lying to me."

"Are we still on for tonight?" Blair asked, changing the subject. Since Robert was supposed to take Cady out on her birthday, they had planned a girl's night out for Saturday night.

"You bet. I'm sure Mr. Jarvis will be with Mom. I'm not sure how much of that I can stomach."

"You mean your mom and dad doing the horizontal mambo."

"Ewww. Saying it out loud is even worse than what is in my head. No kid wants to think their parents are doing that. But no, as long as Isabell is on the hunt for gossip, Mom

69

wouldn't be doing something like that where she could spread the word." They both laughed remembering some of the more salacious tales Isabell had spread around town. "Besides, she didn't bring a man home to meet me until I was in high school."

"Do you know why she never remarried?"

"What do you mean remarried? She was never married in the first place." The bitterness of the last few days came through in her voice. "Sorry. That came out wrong. I don't blame her for the way things turned out. As for your question, she'd dated several men over the years. But I think she's always been in love with Mr. Jarvis. There wasn't room for anyone else."

She didn't know any other explanation for why her mom never married. "Anyway, she knows we're planning on driving into Flagstaff for dinner with the girls and coming back here for the night. You're never too old for a slumber party."

It was Blair's turn to be the designated driver. It wasn't that far from Tumbleweed to Flagstaff, but they wouldn't risk getting in an accident after even having one glass of wine. Since they were celebrating Cady's birthday, she got to have wine.

The four girls had been friends since high school. Their conversation centered on someone shooting at Cady and Deputy Flanagan. Mason Jarvis never came up in conversation. The fact that he was her bio-dad hadn't hit the grapevine yet. She hoped it stayed that way.

It was after nine when the four women piled into Blair's Jeep. The highway was dark and the chance of wildlife on the road could make the trip hazardous. But it wasn't wildlife that had Blair worried now. "Stop singing," Blair shouted over the voices of the others. "Make sure your seat belts are on and tight."

She'd been watching the vehicle behind them for the last five minutes. The driver would get close and then back off, only to get on her bumper again. She could tell it was a big pickup truck by the height of the headlights in her mirror. It didn't help that the guy was using his high beams, nearly blinding her.

"Hang on. I think he's going to ram us. Someone call 911. By the time we need them, we might not be able to call." They jerked against the seatbelt restraints as the truck struck the Jeep from behind.

"Is he drunk?" Jill, one of the girls, asked. She looked out the back window. "He's coming closer again. Can you get off the road? Maybe he won't follow you."

Blair shook her head. "He has more clearance than my Jeep. Nothing's going to stop him from following us. Besides, if we get stuck, we're fair game for whatever he has planned." The thought of what this guy was going to do caused her stomach to churn. She tried slowing down to let the truck get ahead of them, but he matched their speed while still easing closer. Outrunning the truck wasn't going to happen either.

"The 911 operator notified the State Troopers and the sheriff's office." Jill's voice quivered. "Does anyone remember what mile marker we're close to?" There was a chorus of no's. "I told her we left Flagstaff about a half-hour ago, and we're going to Tumbleweed. Hopefully, the cops get here soon or we're toast."

The big truck came up beside them, easing closer until the big side mirror on the truck hit Blair's window causing her to jerk the steering wheel to the right. They bumped over the rough ground. If they'd been in a passenger car, they would have been in even more trouble. She was left with little option but to pull further off the road to avoid being sideswiped again. It wasn't ideal, but it was better than having the heavy truck hit them hard enough to cause them to roll.

"You might want to brace for another hit," she warned. The truck had pulled behind them again. She had to turn her rearview mirror to the side to keep his headlights from wiping out her night vision. Still, she could tell he was getting closer. Just when she thought he was going to ram them, she pressed the gas pedal to the floor. Her Jeep leaped forward in time to avoid the worst of the hit.

Her trick served to incense the other driver. Pulling alongside them again, he swerved, deliberately hitting the Jeep. Blair had been expecting that maneuver. This time she hit the brakes instead of the gas. Instead of being completely broadsided, only the front fender got hit.

"Nice move," Jill complimented her. But she spoke too soon. Whoever was driving the truck was determined to make them crash. He obviously didn't care what kind of damage there was to his truck. Blair was unable to avoid the big truck when it rammed them a second time. The Jeep lurched onto its side, rolling into the ditch at the side of the road.

If not for calling 911 when this started, their situation would have been much worse. Sirens could be heard in the distance within minutes of the Jeep rolling onto its side. Cady heard the roar of the big truck's engine and the smell of burning rubber when it pulled out of the ditch back onto the highway. With the State Troopers so close, their attacker wasn't sticking around. Once again her birthday celebration had turned into a fiasco.

For the next few hours, the four women were shuttled between X-Ray rooms and examining rooms while they waited for the results. The worst of their injuries were mild concussions and numerous cuts and bruises. Blair's Jeep was equipped with every piece of safety equipment possible but she was sure it was totaled.

Tears welled up in Cady's eyes when her mom walked into the examination room where she was waiting for the results of all the X-Rays. When Mason Jarvis followed Olivia, Cady couldn't stop the groan from escaping her lips. This night had been bad enough. Did she also have to deal with him? She'd been hoping her mom would leave him out of it. No such luck.

The slumber party had to be put off for another day. All Cady wanted to do was go home and sleep in her bed. They were all going to be sore in the morning, but at least they were in one piece. Olivia had ordered a birthday cake to celebrate her twenty-first birthday with their church family. She'd missed out on two birthday celebrations, Cady was determined she wouldn't miss the one at church.

CHAPTER EIGHT

"Are you sure you want to go to church this morning?" Olivia asked Cady for the third time since she came down for breakfast. "Yes, Mom, I'm sure. I need to move around or I'll be too stiff to move tomorrow." She picked up the bottle of ibuprofen and dumped two caplets into her hand. She'd feel better once they took effect.

People crowded around the four girls when they limped up to the church entrance a short time later. Everyone was speaking at once wanting to know what happened. News of them being run off the road had already reached the town 'Tell-a-Woman' hotline, meaning Isabell had embellished the results of the crash. "We thought you had died in that crash," one person said. While another wanted to know if they were being cited for drunk driving.

"No one was drunk, and no one died," Cady insisted over all the noise. "If anyone was drunk it was the driver of the pickup. He left the scene before the State Troopers got there." She hoped that would be the end of the questions. The slight concussion made her head feel like there was a drummer pounding inside her head.

A hushed buzz started at the back of the church, and Cady looked over her shoulder to see what was happening. Groaning, she leaned close to Olivia. "What's *he* doing here?"

"He's here for church, the same as everyone else." She patted Cady's hand. "Don't worry. He isn't going to make a scene."

"Maybe not, but someone else will." She nodded at Isabell. She was already making her way over to Mason. The bright glint in her eyes said she could smell fresh gossip as she zeroed in on him. It hadn't taken long for the word to spread through town that the owner of the newest Jarvis House Hotel was in town. His limo had been seen outside Olivia's house several times. How long before they got wind of his relationship with her and Cady?

Everyone was staring at the tall stranger. Looking around, Pastor Bryan saw that Isabell was heading in the man's direction. He'd spoken to her several times about gossiping. So far to no avail. He moved to intercept her. "Good morning, Isabell. Could I have a moment of your time before the service begins?"

"Um, I was just going to greet a visitor. You always say we need to welcome the strangers in our midst." A smug smile lifted one corner of her lips at being able to remind the pastor of Scripture. He couldn't very well deny her that privilege when he'd preached on the subject several times.

"Yes, that is very important, but with the birthday celebration this morning, I want to make sure everything is ready." With a slight nod of his head at Olivia and Cady, he tried to edge Isabell away.

Indecision played across her lined face. Did she go with the pastor, or insist on meeting the man with Olivia? She was determined to finding out what he was to her and Cady.

Pastor Bryan took her arm. "It will only take a minute. I have a big favor to ask of you."

"Oh, all right." She grudgingly gave in, allowing him to lead her away. As they walked toward the kitchen, she looked over her shoulder. The look of relief on Olivia's face was obvious. She knew what Isabell was up to. With a slight growl, she followed the pastor to the kitchen.

"Did you say something, Isabell?" Pastor Bryan asked mildly. "Is something wrong?"

"No, everything is fine," she said through gritted teeth. "What is it you wanted to discuss? I must get back to the sanctuary before the service starts."

"Oh, it won't start without me," he chuckled. "I was wondering if you could take Stella's place cutting the cake this morning."

"Why? What's wrong with Stella doing it?" The women of the congregation took turns serving cake and lemonade at all of the celebrations. This Sunday it was Stella's turn. It didn't matter to Isabell that Stella's daughter had just been in an accident.

"Nothing. I just thought it would be nice if you could take over for her. After the accident the girls were in last night, I'm sure she is still worried about Jill and the others."

"But that would mean I'd have to leave before the service is over," she whined. Her chance to corner Mason Jarvis was slipping through her fingers.

"Yes, I'm sure Stella will be so grateful to you for your kindness."

Unable to think of a way to deny the pastor his request, Isabell finally gave in. "Oh, all right," she grudgingly agreed. "I'll take care of everything." She would make sure some of her ladies would take over for her. They wouldn't deny her this opportunity to gather information.

"That is so kind of you. I know everyone appreciates all you do for our church. You are so organized. I never have to worry about things being amiss when you're in charge." He was laying it on a little thick. "I've asked several other ladies to help out as well," he added. "Everyone wants to learn from all of your experience."

Her eyes narrowed suspiciously. Was he mocking her? Would the pastor do something like that? Still, she couldn't help but congratulate herself on his compliment. After all, she was very organized. "I'm always willing to help out whenever I can." Who would he have helping her? She was certain it wouldn't be the ladies she could bully into taking her place.

"Now we need to head back to the sanctuary. As you said,

we don't want the service to start without us." He chuckled.

Isabell didn't need to be told twice as she hustled out of the kitchen. He wasn't fooling her for a minute. He simply didn't want her to find out what the owner of Jarvis House Hotels was doing with Olivia and Cady. Just because she was stuck behind the table passing out cake, lemonade, and coffee didn't mean she wouldn't be able to talk to the man. No one was going to stop her from getting the low down on his relationship with Olivia.

She was tired of the pastor calling her interest in the people of the church and town gossip. Gossip was a sin, and she would never do something like that. She was better than he gave her credit for being. With her head held high, she walked into the sanctuary.

Following slowly in her wake, Pastor Bryan shook his head. Someday Isabell's gossiping would get her in trouble. He'd only put off the inevitable though. Very little would keep her from her objective. She wanted to know what Mason Jarvis was doing with Olivia and Cady.

At least, they would be able to have a few minutes with their friends while Isabell was making sure everyone has something to eat and drink. She wouldn't want it to be said that something went wrong on her watch.

Before proceeding to the front of the church, he stopped to speak to Stella. Her surprise that Isabell had offered to take over cake duty was obvious as she looked to where the older woman was sitting. Isabell never helped out unless there was something in it for her. What was she up to this time?

Still, she was grateful. She offered Isabell a watery smile when the woman looked her way. It had been a harrowing night for all four families when they learned their daughters had been run off the road by a hit-and-run driver.

Isabell wasn't the only one eager to meet Mason Jarvis. As owner of the newest and best hotel in town, he was sort of a celebrity in their small town. He suspected few people in the congregation paid attention to the sermon. They were paying more attention to the handsome man sitting with Olivia and Cady. He had to admit he was curious. But if Olivia wanted him to know anything, she would tell him. He wouldn't ask.

As the service ended, Pastor Bryan stopped at the row where the families were seated together. Taking in the injuries of the four young women, he leaned over. "We all heard about your accident. I'm so grateful your injuries aren't more serious. Would you all like to follow me out to the courtyard to get started on the birthday celebration? I think there is a lot to be thankful for this morning." During the service, he had offered prayers of thanks that they hadn't been seriously injured and for a speedy recovery for them all.

Once outside, he held out his hand to Mason, smiling up at the much taller man. "Welcome to Tumbleweed Church. I'm Pastor Bryan McCullum."

"Nice to meet you, Pastor." Looking over the pastor's shoulder, he leaned a little closer. "Thanks for intervening earlier." They were standing beside a table far enough away from the refreshment table that Isabell couldn't hear what they were saying.

The pastor chuckled. "My pleasure." He turned to the four girls. "I'm glad you're all doing okay. I heard some horrific stories about your experience."

"Yes, I'm sure you have." They all looked to where Isabell was passing out cake. She was watching them with intense interest. "Most of those stories were probably exaggerated far beyond the truth," Jill said. "Thankfully, Blair had taken that defensive driver course. She saved us from any worse injuries." Thinking about what the driver of the truck might have done if the State Troopers hadn't gotten there so fast made her shudder.

Spotting Deputy Flanagan at the edge of the crowd, Cady

excused herself and made her way over to him. "I'm sure you aren't here to wish me happy birthday."

Touching the brim of his big cowboy hat, he shook his head. "Sorry to be interrupting, but I wanted to check up on you. How are you doing? I read the report. It sounds like you were lucky, sorry," he chuckled. "I mean you were blessed when the State Troopers arrived so quickly."

"Blessed and thankful." She nodded. "When Blair realized the guy was going to run us off the road, she made sure we were all buckled in and one of us called 911. I'm not sure what the guy had in mind for us, but things would have been a lot worse if the state troopers hadn't shown up when they did." A shudder wracked her body at the memory of the accident.

"Were any of you able to describe the truck? Could you see who was driving?" He knew it was a long shot, but he could still hope.

The officers at the scene had asked the same thing. No one had been able to describe the truck or driver. She shook her head slowly to avoid rattling her brain any more than it already was. "No, the windows were all tinted so dark we couldn't see who was driving." A frown pulled her brows into a V between her dark eyes.

"What?" Darrell prompted. He could read her expressive face. "You remembered something."

She tilted her head to one side. "I don't know if it's a memory of the accident or something from a movie." She was silent for a moment as she tried to make sense of what was in her mind. "It was like the Joker in the Batman movies."

"What was like the Joker?" He was confused.

"Just before the Jeep flipped, I saw the person in the truck. In the greenish glow from the dashboard lights, his face was distorted. It was like a ghoul was looking at me. Was that for real or just something I conjured up because I was scared?"

He shook his head. "I'm not sure. Our minds can play

tricks on us. I'm glad you weren't seriously hurt. If you remember anything else, give me a call." He handed her another card in case she'd lost the first one.

He started to turn away when Cady stopped him. "Would you like some cake and lemonade or coffee?" she asked hopefully.

His smile filled his face and her heart. "I guess I can spare a few minutes." He followed her across the patio.

Keeping an eye on all the players was easier than Isabell expected. From her vantage point at the refreshment table, she was able to watch everyone. She would love to hear what Olivia was saying when people approached her. How was she explaining Mason Jarvis's sudden appearance at her house? She knew there was a story there. If it was the last thing she did, she was going to find out what that story was.

Little did she realize how prophetic that thought was.

"How are things going, Isabell?" Pastor Bryan stepped into her line of sight. "You're doing an excellent job as always."

"Yes, of course." She accepted the compliment as her due. She tipped her head to the side to look around him. Cady had left the table where she'd been sitting. Where was she going? Trying to follow with her eyes, the pastor shifted his stance obstructing her view again.

"You know that old saying about curiosity and cats, don't you, Isabell?"

She frowned at him. What was he prattling on about now? "No, I'm sorry I don't know what you mean." Distracted, she wasn't paying attention to what he was saying.

"Curiosity killed the cat," he quoted.

"And satisfaction brought him back," she answered smugly, proud that she'd been able to best him.

"Not always, Isabell, not always. You might want to remember that."

"Are you implying something? I don't think pastors should

80

go around making threats." She puffed up with self-importance.

"It wasn't a threat, Isabell. It was a word of caution. Getting into other people's business isn't ever wise."

"You have nothing to worry about. I'm always cautious." She picked up a plate with a large piece of cake. "Would you care for another piece of cake? I know how much you like your sweets."

"No, thank you. One piece was more than enough." He walked off shaking his head. How long before someone took offense to her prying into their business and did something everyone would regret.

CHAPTER NINE

Robert watched from the shadows across the street as people crowded around Mason. "They're falling all over that guy like he's a rock star or something," he muttered. "If they knew the truth about him and his hussy whore, they'd change their minds."

After Jarvis kicked him out of his own hotel, it had been necessary to keep a low profile. He figured that deputy had already been to his apartment. What had Cady said about him? "She's no better than her mother," he muttered. "She has that deputy wrapped around her little finger." He was lucky he hadn't fallen for her charms.

The nosy bitch passing out cake had tried to corner him before he'd been able to find a safe place to stay while still being able to keep an eye on things. An evil grin lit up his face as an idea took shape in his mind. If the old biddy was looking for dirt on Jarvis, he could give her an earful. Turning away, he contemplated how to go about doing that while avoiding her questions.

"Thank you for taking over for me this morning." Stella cautiously approached Isabell. She'd been on the receiving end of the older woman's daggers all morning. Everyone in town knew Isabell wanted to be where the action was and that wasn't being stuck behind the table passing out cake and drinks. She would rather be moving from group to group listening for any gossip. *She wouldn't hear any at their table,* Stella thought. Olivia had introduced Mr. Jarvis as an acquaintance from college, nothing else.

"As you can imagine, I don't want to leave Jill out of my sight after what happened last night. We were so worried about her and the others when we got the call about the accident."

"Oh, I know," Isabell gushed with false sympathy. "I can imagine how worried you must have been." Isabell's tone was sweet enough to decay teeth. If she worked this right, she might be able to learn what the girls had talked about over drinks. Everyone knew drinking loosened lips. "I'm sure you were very worried, as any parent would be. What did Jill say about the accident?"

If she couldn't get the scoop on Mason Jarvis, she would take this opportunity to find out what she could about the accident. So far, the police were saying very little other than a hit and run driver ran them off the road. She was sure there was more to it than that. This was the second time Cady's life had been in jeopardy. Things had certainly heated up since Mason Jarvis came to town. She was mentally rubbing her hands together in glee.

"That monster deliberately ran them off the road." Stella's voice quivered as she interrupted Isabell's thoughts. "If the police hadn't shown up as fast as they did..." Tears brimmed in her eyes at the thought of what that man had been planning on doing to the girls.

"Oh, I'm sure he wasn't going to hurt *all* of them." Her implication was clear. "Maybe he was only after one of them?" Her voice trailed up at the end as an invitation for Stella to add more information.

"What are you suggesting? Why would he single out one over the others?" Stella frowned. "Those girls hadn't done anything wrong."

"Oh, no, that's not what I meant." She backpedaled quickly. "I heard they were celebrating Cady's birthday. Maybe something happened at the club they went to. One never can tell what will happen at places like that." She shook her head sadly. "Maybe they had too much to drink and weren't aware they cut the other driver off. There is a lot of road rage happening."

Stella's back stiffened. "When the girls go out together, they always have a designated driver who doesn't drink. Thanks again for taking over the refreshment table." Without another word, Stella spun away before she picked up what remained of the cake and smashed it in Isabell's face. The woman was insufferable.

Isabell gave a huffy sniff. That didn't give her what she was looking for. She was sure Cady had told them why Mason Jarvis was in town and what connection he had to her and Olivia.

The crowd was beginning to thin out and she still hadn't been able to talk to Mason Jarvis. There was still clean-up to be done. If she wasn't careful, the opportunity would slip away altogether. Looking around, she snarled softly. Her so-called helpers had already deserted her, leaving her to clean up on her own. She hated the fact that she was stuck serving a bunch of ungrateful people while they hobnobbed with the likes of Mason Jarvis.

Across the patio, the four girls were huddled together whispering all sorts of juicy tidbits. If she could have just a minute with one of them, she might be able to learn why that man was in town. She was becoming obsessed with learning what he had to do with Olivia and Cady Townsend.

One good thing had come from being stuck on the sidelines. She'd seen Cady with that handsome new deputy. She was sure something was going on there. Was he the reason Cady had dumped Robert Gaston? She'd heard that Mason Jarvis had fired him. What was that about? Mason Jarvis breezes into town and all sorts of exciting things happen in their normally dull town.

It's no wonder he didn't want to talk to me, she thought. *The poor man,* she tsked softly. *No one wants to admit they've been jilted. Did Mason Jarvis' sudden appearance have anything to do with Cady dumping him?* There had to be a connection.

She continued considering her options. The other employees at the hotel had been unwilling to discuss why he had been fired. Why were people being so closed mouth all of a sudden? Maybe it was time to have dinner at that fancy restaurant.

Minutes later, any chance to talk to Mason Jarvis disappeared altogether as the group made their way to the parking lot where the big limousine was parked. Well, she wasn't going to let him escape that easily, she silently vowed. People in this town called her the queen of information for a reason. That wasn't the real name folks called her, but she preferred the slant she'd given the name. If there was anything to be found out about anyone, she was the person to find it.

Someone had tried to kill Cady twice. Wasn't it her duty to figure out why before someone was accidentally killed along with Cady? The night before proved it was a very real possibility. She was surprised Stella hadn't been more forthcoming. Did she want her daughter to be caught in the crossfire?

Leaning her head against the backrest, Cady breathed a sigh of relief. Maybe she should have foregone the birthday celebration as her mom wanted. She hurt in places she didn't know she had. Each passing hour increased the aches and pains. She had a bright purple bruise across her chest from the seatbelt harness. It might have saved her from worse injuries, but it also caused other injuries. X-rays showed that she had a bone bruise on her sternum from the harness. All she wanted to do now was to go home and sleep for the next week.

When the big limo pulled to a stop behind Olivia's car, Cady knew sleep wasn't going to happen right away. She had a few questions for him, and she was sure he would be asking her the same questions the State Troopers had asked the night before and Deputy Flanagan asked this morning. There wasn't anything else to tell them.

"Why does he insist on going everywhere in a limo?" she softly asked Olivia as she carefully made her way out of the car. "It's like a neon sign pointing to where he is every minute. Doesn't he drive?"

"Of course he does, dear." She paused. "Well, I'm assuming he still does. When I knew him, he drove part of the time. Having a driver allows him time to get work done instead of wasting time sitting in traffic."

"Unless he's working while he's here, it might be a good idea for him to ditch the limo. Isabell was chomping at the bit to corner him. He'd have an easier time avoiding her if she didn't know exactly where he was every minute of the day." Without waiting for her mom, she headed for the house.

Stepping into the living room, she moaned with pleasure at the aroma filling the house. Before leaving for church, Olivia had put a large dish in the oven with Cady's favorite food; cheese enchiladas with green chilis. After having a large slice of cake, she told herself that she wasn't hungry. But her stomach wasn't listening. Peeking into the oven, her stomach rumbled at the delicious aroma coming from the bubbling sauce and cheese.

"Wow, something smells delicious," Mason commented as he followed Olivia into the living room. He sniffed the air. "I'll bet it's something with green chilis. Am I right?" He cocked his head at her, a teasing grin lifting one corner of his full lips.

A breath caught in Olivia's throat. She'd seen that same look on her daughter's face more times than she could count in the last twenty-one years. She turned away to hide the tears that burned at the back of her eyes. They had all missed so much.

"We just had cake and lemonade. The enchiladas will be done by the time I have the table set. I set the temperature on low before we left home. Keep the door closed so they will finish cooking." She chuckled at her daughter's look of disappointment only to turn and see the identical look on Mason's face.

An awkward silence filled the room as they all sat down. Cady had a lot of questions, but where did she start? "Did you talk to Robert about spying on me?" That question was far down on her list when it popped out of her mouth. She watched him for any sign of complicity in his expression.

"Yes, and of course he denied knowing what I was talking about. He tried to play dumb, that he didn't know you are my daughter. I didn't believe that any more than the other things he said."

He ran his long fingers through his dark hair. He kept it cut short to prevent the unruly curls from forming. He couldn't help but smile when he noticed that Cady had inherited her curls and dark hair from him. "He said the hotel here in Tumbleweed belongs to him. He's planning on toppling my hotel empire, as he called it. According to Robert, Jerrod signed everything concerning the hotel here over to him." Olivia gasped, and he squeezed her hand reassuringly. "Of course, that won't hold up in court since Jerrod isn't authorized to sign anything concerning the company."

"Where's Robert now?" Cady asked. "Does he still work for you?"

Mason gave a harsh laugh. "Not a chance. He was smart enough to take me at my word when I gave him an hour to remove his personal items and leave. I made sure there was security with him while he cleaned out his office."

"Is he still in town?"

Mason shrugged. "Unfortunately, I don't have the power to make him leave town. If he's smart though, he will leave."

"Why would Jerrod sign the hotel over to him?" Olivia asked softly. She could see the hurt Jerrod's betrayal caused

Mason.

"Because he hates me," he answered simply. "But more than that, Robert is his cousin. I was unaware of that when he was hired or he never would have made it past the application stage. His mother and my late wife were sisters." He gave them the Cliff Notes version of what he'd learned from Robert.

"He claims he has papers proving that I stole the company from his grandpa. I have papers proving otherwise. For years I gave that family money every time they asked. It wasn't until after you were born," he looked at Cady, "that I finally cut them off. I had better uses for that money. I couldn't stop Belinda from sending them money though."

"Do you think Robert is behind the shooting and running the girls off the road last night?" If that was the case, they needed to tell the sheriff's department.

"I don't know what he's capable of." He shook his head. "I have spoken with that deputy who brought Cady home the other night. He said he would keep an eye on her to make sure she's safe." He gave Cady a crooked smile. "I saw him at the church this morning. I think he's sweet on you."

Cady's face got warm. She hoped he was right. But what did it matter to Mason whether Darrell was sweet on her? It was none of his business. The timer on the oven went off, and she breathed a relieved sigh. *Saved by the bell,* she thought.

CHAPTER TEN

Much to Cady's dismay, it didn't appear that Mason was going away any time soon. She wasn't sure what running a large hotel chain entailed, but it seemed he was able to conduct business from Tumbleweed without any problem. The threats Robert had issued hadn't materialized. Olivia invited him to dinner every evening, even when Cady wasn't going to be there. He was making an effort to get to know her and she couldn't decide how she felt about that.

When Deputy Darrell came into the library the following morning, butterflies fluttered in Cady's stomach. She'd been hoping to see him again, but not if it was concerning the accident or someone shooting at her. "The truck that ran you off the road was found," he told her. That wasn't what she wanted him to say, but it would have to do.

"Did you arrest the owner?"

"Sorry." He shook his head. "It had been reported stolen the day before the accident. Without any kind of description at the time of the accident, we weren't able to tie the two things together. Forensics has found paint transferred from the Jeep on the truck. There was also matching paint from the truck on the Jeep."

"Were you able to pull any fingerprints off the truck?" she asked hopefully.

Darrell shook his head. "Either the guy wore gloves or was able to clean everything he touched. The only prints they found belonged to the owner or his family."

"Are you sure the owner isn't lying? Maybe he ran us off the road and reported the truck stolen to cover it up."

Darrell shook his head. He wished he had better news. "At the time someone was running you girls off the road, he and his family were at a party in Flagstaff."

"So, another dead end," Cady sighed. There hadn't been any usable fingerprints on the shell casings, and the gun used to shoot at her hadn't been used in any other crimes. It was going to take some good luck, or blessings, to catch this guy. She hoped that happened before there was another attempt on her life.

There wasn't anything else to say, but he wasn't in a hurry to leave. He wanted to ask her out, but she had enough going on in her life. Maybe this wasn't a good time. "Well, I'll let you get back to work. I wanted to let you know the truck had been found. I wish it was better news."

"Me, too." When he continued to hesitate, she held her breath, hoping he would ask her out.

"Maybe I'll see you later?" It was a question. Just not the question she'd been hoping for.

"I'd like that."

His twin dimples winked at her when he smiled. "Good. I'll give you a call." There was a spring in his step as he left the library.

Darrell had just left when Isabell came up to Cady's desk. She was early for her book club meeting. That could only mean one thing. She was there on a fishing expedition. "Good morning, Cady." She smiled sweetly down on her. "How are you feeling after your harrowing experience last week? I never got a chance to wish you a happy birthday on Sunday before you escaped."

"Thank you, Isabell. I'm doing much better. I'm sorry I didn't have a chance to talk to you. But as you can imagine, we were all still shook up and hurting after what happened. Our guardian angels had been with us the night before. What book are you planning on reviewing this week?" Switching topics when Isabell was on a mission to get information didn't always work, but she had to try.

"Oh, we'll have to figure that out when everyone gets here.

I have a few minutes to spare so I came early so I could visit with you."

Cady groaned softly. That meant Isabell was there to grill her about Mason. So far, no one in town had picked up on the fact that he was her father. She wasn't certain how that had slipped by. But she was grateful all the same.

Before Isabell had a chance to pry further, a man stepped up behind her. When Isabell ignored the fact that he was waiting to talk to Cady, he tapped his foot impatiently. "I'm sorry, Isabell. I think this gentleman needs some assistance." Cady cut her off before she could ask any more questions. She stepped away in a huff, but she didn't go far. She fully intended to continue her conversation with Cady when he left.

"Is there something I can help you with, Sir?" He was well over six feet tall, in his late twenties or early thirties with blonde hair and light-colored eyes. Newcomers came into the library on a regular basis looking for help finding information about the town.

Before answering, he looked at Isabell where she was standing only a few feet away. "Do you mind? This is a private conversation."

"Well, I never," she huffed. Taking several steps away from Cady's desk, she was still within eavesdropping distance. If this was private, she had every intention of knowing what he wanted.

"I'm sure you haven't, lady. Maybe this should be the first time. Butt out of my business."

"Sir, that isn't necessary. We can step over here." Cady stood up, taking several steps away from her desk. Looking over her shoulder at Isabell, she said, "You'll have to excuse us. I'll talk to you later." There was little the older woman could do but stay where she was while Cady led the young man out of her hearing.

She turned to look at the man. "Now, what is it you need

help with?" She was getting a bad feeling about him.

"Do you know who I am?"

Cady frowned. "No. How would I know that? I've never seen you before."

"I'm Jerrod Jarvis, your half-brother."

Her face lost all color, and she staggered back several steps as though he'd struck her.

"Cady, are you all right?" Isabell had moved close to Cady's desk hoping to be able to hear what they were saying. "What did he do to you?" Her sharp voice echoed around the high ceiling causing other library visitors to look up. "Should I call 911?" She had no intention of calling the sheriff before she found out who he was and what he was doing in her town. She didn't know what was happening, but she could make something up to go along with the action.

"No, Isabell. I'm fine. Go have a seat with your book club." It wasn't time for the other ladies to arrive, but she didn't want the woman to hear what Jerrod had to say. "Let's go into the workroom where we can talk privately."

"Good idea," he said. "I'm sure you don't want what I have to say to get out."

Acid churned in Cady's stomach. Why was he here? What was he going to do? Surely, he wouldn't attack her. There were too many people aware that he'd said something to upset her. Her cell phone was in her pocket. After the two attempts to harm her, she'd taken to keeping it with her at all times. She wasn't sure whether she could call 911 on the sly though. He would be close enough to stop her from calling for help.

With the door to the small workroom closed, she whirled around to face him. "What do you want?"

He shrugged. "I wanted to meet my half-sister and see what a gold digger looks like."

"All right, you met me. I'm sorry to disappoint you, but I'm not a gold digger. I have no claim on anything belonging to your father. Nor do I want to. Where were you Friday and Saturday of last week?" She turned the table on him.

"I was in San Francisco. What difference does it make to you?" A dark frown drew his brows together.

"Those are the nights someone tried to kill me along with three of my friends. You wouldn't happen to know something about that, would you?"

"What? I didn't try to kill you."

"So you say. Yet here you are making absurd accusations against me. Can you prove you weren't here, or that you didn't pay someone to try to kill me?" The best defense is a good offense.

"I was with friends on those nights and... Wait a minute; I don't have to prove anything to you."

"That's right you don't. But I'm sure the sheriff's department would be interested in hearing what you have to say. I have the number right here." She pulled her phone out of her pocket. She'd programmed Darrell Flanagan's number into her phone after what happened Saturday night. She wanted to be sure she could reach someone quickly.

"Hold on a minute. I didn't try to kill you. I wouldn't do something like that."

"Fine." She took a deep breath. "You've accomplished your mission. You've seen me. You need to leave. Now. Go see your father. I'm sure he has some things to say to you about your cousin Robert." She opened the door, stepping aside for him to leave. She was still holding her phone. If he didn't leave, she would call Darrell.

With little choice but to leave or have a talk with the police, Jerrod walked out of the workroom. He could feel the old biddy watching him as he walked out of the small room. But she wasn't the only one. Everyone in the library was now watching to see what was going to happen next.

That hadn't turned out the way he'd planned. The next

conversation was going to be even worse. After the scene at his mother's funeral, his father probably didn't want to see him either. If what that woman said was true and someone had tried to kill her, he was sure his dad was going to blame him or Melanie for what happened. His dad had tried to protect him and his sister when they were growing up. *Until they'd proven they weren't worth protecting*, he thought with a sigh. Maybe the way things turned out wasn't entirely his dad's fault.

CHAPTER ELEVEN

Had someone really tried to kill her? Who would do something like that? His old man would probably blame him for that, he silently groused. Lost in his thoughts, Jerrod didn't see the man coming in as he headed for the door. He took a step back. "Excuse…" Seeing who was standing in front of him, he whirled around. "You bitch! You called the cops." He took a menacing step toward Cady.

"Hold it right there." Darrell barked out the order. His hand was on the butt of his gun just in case the man didn't take him seriously.

Isabell was dancing with glee at having a front-row seat to the action. She didn't know who the man was, but this was bound to get interesting.

"I didn't do anything to her," Jerrod snapped. "Why'd you call the cops?"

"I didn't." Cady looked around at the people seated at the different tables. She didn't think Isabell had either. She was enjoying this way too much to want it to stop.

Wayne Westin, a high school senior studying for his SATs, held up his phone. "I called. You looked like you were ready to strangle Miss Cady. I wasn't going to let that happen." He stood up. At five feet ten and barely a hundred and fifty pounds soaking wet, he didn't look like he could wrestle a good-sized dog and win. But he wasn't going to let a stranger hurt one of their own.

"I wasn't gonna hurt her." Jerrod took a menacing step toward the young boy.

"I said to hold it right there," Darrell ordered again. "I think it would be a good idea for us to go somewhere that we can sort this out in private."

"No." Isabell wasn't aware she'd spoken out loud until

95

everyone turned to stare at her. "Um, I mean, we're all witnesses to what happened. Don't you want to question me, us?"

"I'll get back to you on that, Mrs. Brewster. Let's go down to the station and have a little chat." Jerrod was still protesting when Darrell led him out of the library.

Isabell's face fell with disappointment. How was she ever going to find out what was going on when everything happened behind closed doors?

"Oh, Cady, I was so scared for you. Do you know that guy? What did he want? Why would he try to harm you? Is he the one that shot at you and ran you off the road? Did he come here to kill you? Why would he do that?" Isabell's questions spewed out like lava from a volcano.

Cady's legs felt like rubber and she sank down onto her desk chair. Was this nightmare ever going to end? It wasn't even a week since her twenty-first birthday and the surprises just kept coming. So far, none of them had been good surprises.

"Cady. Didn't you hear me?" Isabell gave Cady's shoulder a shake. She didn't like being ignored. "Who is that guy? You need to answer my questions." It never occurred to her that it was none of her business. Everything was her business.

"Leave her alone, Mrs. Brewster." Wayne stepped up to protect Cady from the older woman's ire. He'd had a crush on Cady since he was in junior high school. She wasn't that much older than him. That was why he spent so much time in the library. "Can't you see she's upset?"

"Stay out of this, young man, or I'll call your parents." She didn't like being ignored; she liked even less being told what to do.

Cady turned her attention to the older woman. "No, Isabell, I don't need to answer your questions." Library patrons were beginning to gather around her desk. Everyone wanted in on the excitement. She needed to get this under control. "Thank you, Wayne, for calling the sheriff." She gave him a weak smile. She tried to maintain a civil tone when she looked at Isabell again. "I believe your group is here. Do you need help picking out your next book?"

"B... b... but," she sputtered. "You didn't answer my questions."

"Nor am I going to. If you want answers, you should track down that man. Maybe he'll be willing to satisfy your... curiosity. Now, if you'll excuse me, I need to get back to work." Without another word, she tapped a key on her keyboard to wake her computer up. She had no idea what she'd been working on before Jerrod walked in, but she could fake it.

"Well, I never," Isabell huffed, stomping to the back of the big room.

~~~

Until he could hire a replacement manager, Mason took over running the hotel. The entire hotel had a different feel from the other hotels in his chain. Was that what Jerrod was hoping for? After looking things over, he realized it would be easy enough to make a few changes so the hotel would conform to the other properties.

Before taking over the office, he'd made sure there were no listening devices planted anywhere. All he needed was to have Robert, or someone, listening in on any business taking place. Fortunately, the office had been clean. That was probably because he hadn't given Robert time to do something like that. He sighed. He was beginning to see conspiracies everywhere.

He blamed himself for what Robert had done. He should have paid closer attention to what Belinda and Jerrod were doing. He thought Jerrod was running the hotel as General Manager. Finding out he'd signed over everything to Robert

97

was a knife in his back.

He had planned on staying in Tumbleweed while he got to know his daughter and convinced Olivia there was still something between them. He didn't want to spend all of his time working. He sighed. Nothing was going as he'd hoped when he came here.

He had spent as much time with Olivia and Cady over the weekend as possible. Cady was still angry at the way they had handled everything. But who could blame her? After the accident Saturday night, she had spent most of the afternoon in bed as well as the next day. She hated missing work, but the doctor had ordered all four women to take life easy for a few days.

His attorney had assured him that Robert's threats were baseless. At the time he'd acquired the small motels from his father-in-law, he had made sure everything was above board. He had the old man's signature on every piece of paper. There was no way Robert could claim he'd cheated his grandfather out of his business.

Hindsight is always twenty-twenty, he thought. Looking back on things from the vantage point of time, he figured Belinda and her father had been planning something like this for a long time. The motels were supposed to be a wedding present. Even so, he had insisted on paying the old man for them. If Robert was at all like his grandfather and aunt, this mess wasn't over. It was like waiting for the other shoe to drop.

Mason leaned back in the plush chair. Jerrod had spared no expense when furnishing the offices or the rooms, most of which were suites.

He ran his long fingers through his hair. Jerrod had claimed he wanted to prove himself by doing this one project entirely on his own. Belinda had harped at him until he gave in and allowed Jerrod to set up the entire project. He hadn't even seen the blueprints. The first time he'd seen the hotel was when he came to meet Cady.

The building had a generic look like so many other hotels. That wasn't what he wanted for his brand. His hotels looked more like the bed and breakfasts he'd grown up visiting with his parents.

If Jerrod had been honest instead of working with Robert to take over this hotel, it would have gone a long way to repairing his relationship with his son. Instead, he'd turned it over to his cousin. After this stunt, Mason wasn't sure there was anything left to repair. How would he ever be able to trust him again?

Was he behind the two attempts on Cady's life? Was he so greedy that he wouldn't want his half-sister to have any part of what Mason had built? His trust had been drawn up before he'd even met Belinda, naming any children he had as his main heirs. Belinda would have been taken care of if he'd died before her, but she wasn't a trustee or the executor of his estate. That was why he didn't understand how Robert thought he could get away with this.

He'd missed out on the first twenty-one years of Cady's life because of his wife. He wasn't about to lose her now. Who else would want to harm Cady? Only Jerrod and Melanie would benefit if something happened to her. Melanie had entered yet another rehab facility in an attempt to dry out. He wasn't sure anything would ever work. She had to want to get sober. So far, she didn't want it bad enough.

Unable to sit still, Mason stood up, pacing across the large office. Robert had left the hotel, but had he left Tumbleweed? There was no way he could force him to leave town. He chuckled. *This town ain't big enough for the two of us. It's time for you to git.* It sounded like bad dialogue from a bad western movie. But where was he? Trying to keep Olivia and Cady safe and keep up with work here and his other properties didn't leave a lot of time to track down Robert.

The intercom buzzed interrupting his thoughts. "Yes, what is it?" His terse tone had the woman filling in as his assistant stammering.

"Y... your... s...son w... would like to s...see you, Sir."

"Send him in, and I apologize for snapping at you." He didn't normally treat his employees like that. But he also didn't normally have employees trying to steal his company.

"Y...yes, Sir." She didn't sound quite so afraid he was going to bite off her head. "I'll send him in."

Mason didn't know what to expect out of this visit. After confronting Robert, he'd called Jerrod. He'd barely been able to contain his temper. Jerrod claimed he hadn't signed the hotel over to Robert, and he didn't know anything about Robert's plans to take over the company. He said he'd only recently learned that Robert was his cousin. How much of anything he said was the truth? Now he's here in Tumbleweed. This should be interesting.

At the light tap on the door, he called out for him to come in. It was a better beginning than some of his meetings with his son. Usually, Jerrod would barge into his office uninvited, demanding something from his father. Was this a good sign?

Jerrod looked enough like his mother to cause his stomach to roll. He kept praying it wasn't too late for the boy to acquire some redeeming qualities. *But he's no longer a boy*, he reminded himself, he was a man. Mason sighed. Would things ever change between them?

At the moment, he looked less like his mother and more like the little boy Mason remembered before Belinda turned both of his children against him.

"What can I do for you, Jerrod? I'm surprised to see you here." His emotions were torn between being angry at the man Jerrod had become and wishing for the young boy he'd once been. But that was a long time ago.

"I wanted to tell you I'm sorry. I didn't come here to cause trouble. I came here to meet..." He took a gulping breath before he could continue. "I came here to meet my half-sister," he said, starting over. "I wanted to know if what Mother had said about her and her mother was the truth." He was standing at attention in front of Mason's desk as though he was in the military.

"And what did your mother say about them?" A muscle jumped in his jaw. He could imagine, but he wanted to hear what Jerrod would say. Looking up at his son, he wondered when he'd become so tall. Why hadn't he noticed before? The only thing he'd gotten from his father was his tall slender build.

"It's not worth repeating, Sir."

"You don't have to call me sir. I'm your father, not your commanding officer."

Jerrod nodded, relaxing slightly. "As you know, I met her earlier. I want to apologize to her, but Deputy Flanagan warned me against seeing her again." His lips twitched slightly. "I think he has the hots for her." Saying the words out loud caused him to frown. He wasn't sure how he was supposed to feel about that. There were so many conflicting emotions raging through him he didn't know from one minute to the next how he felt about anything.

"What would you like me to do?" Mason asked.

Jerrod shrugged his broad shoulders. "I guess I'd like you to tell her I'm sorry. I didn't mean to come off as though I was threatening her." For too long he'd hated the thought of Cady and her mother. His mother had nothing nice to say about either of them. Under the circumstances, he couldn't exactly blame her. He was beginning to question a lot of things his mother told him though. He didn't know what to think about his parents and his father's love child.

Drawing another deep breath, he plunged forward with

101

what he was going to say next before he chickened out. "This hotel was supposed to be my opportunity to prove I could handle things without you breathing down my neck. I'm not completely incompetent." He couldn't stop the bitterness from creeping back into his voice.

"I never said you were. Your mother taught you to take without ever giving anything back. You can't blame me for being skeptical of your motives." He paused. "After hearing what Robert was planning, I still am."

Jerrod's face got red at that. His mother had been pulling the strings on this project and everything else he'd ever tried to do. "Mother said the company would belong to me someday, but you never trusted me with anything." He resented that as much as anything else his father had ever done.

"You never took the initiative to learn what it takes to run a company of any size, let alone one this size," Mason said. "You can't sit around doing nothing and expect to be handed everything at the end of the day. When you asked if you could be in charge of building one hotel, I was hoping you had finally taken an interest in learning what it takes to run a company, any company. I should have known better. This hotel doesn't fit our brand. What were you thinking?"

Jerrod looked like he was ready to explode, but he didn't argue. "The truth is a hard pill to swallow, Son," Mason stated mildly. "Did you know Olivia and Cady lived in Tumbleweed when you chose to build here?" Jerrod shook his head, but he didn't explain. "Then how did you come to pick this town?"

With a heavy sigh, Jerrod flopped into one of the plush chairs in front of the desk. "This was where Mother wanted the hotel to be. I didn't understand why it was so important to her. I tried to tell her the type of hotels in our chain would never make it in such a small town." He rubbed at a small scar at one corner of his mouth.

At the time, Mason had wondered how he'd gotten the scar.

Now he knew. Belinda had lashed out at him when he didn't immediately comply with her wishes. He should have paid closer attention to what was happening at home a long time ago. The way his children had turned out was as much his fault as it was Belinda's.

"So you went along with what she wanted." It wasn't a question. He couldn't blame Jerrod for doing what he'd done all these years. Belinda wasn't the type to take opposition lightly.

"It was easier to go along with what she wanted than to try fighting her," Jerrod admitted. "She'd win anyway." He was beginning to see why his father had cheated. What he didn't understand was why he hadn't gotten a divorce?

"If you never loved Mother, why did you marry her? I know she was pregnant, but that is no reason to marry someone you don't love. Why didn't you get a divorce later? Wouldn't that have been easier than fighting at every turn?" He hadn't come here to ask his father about his marriage. The questions had just slipped out.

Mason sighed. These were some hard truths for Jerrod to hear and even harder for him to admit. "Nothing was ever easy with your mother," he said with a weary sigh. "I'm not sure I ever loved her. But if I did, that love never made it past the first year. Our marriage was more of convenience than love almost from the start. She changed after we were married. I had just acquired a franchise for a hotel when I met your mother. Belinda saw me as a ticket out of a bad situation at home. I had big plans, but I never expected to build what I have today."

His voice was quiet as he continued, his thoughts lost somewhere in the past. "I tried to make things work, but eventually I realized she wasn't interested in making that happen. By that time we had two kids to think about. It was just easier to stay married than to fight for a divorce. She would have taken everything I had worked to build." Their marriage had been a struggle from day one.

"So it was all about money," Jerrod's bitter voice brought his thoughts back to the present. "And you accuse me of only wanting money." He shook his head. "You said your love didn't last. Was that because you cheated on her? That's why she hated you."

Mason shook his head. "I never cheated on your mother until I met Olivia. That's when I realized again what love really was."

"Ha," Jerrod snorted, clearly not believing his father. "You're saying you never strayed even though you and Mother hated each other. I don't believe that. Why would you do that? Don't tell me you stayed together "for the kids"," He placed air quotes around the last words. "As far back as I can remember Mother hated when you went on one of your many business trips. She knew you would be with other women while you were gone. Melanie and I were the ones that suffered for what you did."

"I don't care whether you believe me or not. The only woman I have ever been with besides your mother was Olivia," he stressed again.

"So why not get a divorce?" He still didn't understand.

"Because Belinda threatened to kill Olivia and our unborn child if I left, then she would kill you and Melanie and herself." He hadn't meant to ever tell his children that about their mother, but Jerrod had kept pushing.

"She would never do something like that," Jerrod scoffed. "She was mean, but she wasn't a killer."

"That wasn't a chance I was willing to take. I needed to protect you and your sister as well as Olivia. It wasn't until years later that I discovered Belinda had hired a private investigator to find Olivia and Cady." They were getting far off the topic but maybe they both needed to say and hear these things. "How did Robert become the manager at this hotel? I thought that was what you wanted. You said you didn't find out he was your cousin until much later."

They'd had very little contact with Belinda's family after they were married. At least that was what Belinda wanted him to believe. She'd gone behind his back on so many things. If only he could go back and do things differently, he would. But there was no going back, only going forward.

Jerrod nodded. "I met Robert several years ago. He was working at one of the smaller hotels in the San Francisco area. Mother encouraged our friendship." He snorted. "That should have been my first clue. She'd never liked any of my friends before. He said he'd worked for a small construction company in the town where he grew up, and he was trying to branch out into something with a better future.

"When he found out about this project, he asked to be let in on it. He could help out on the construction end and then work his way into management once the hotel was built. I thought I was doing him a favor by giving him a job. Everything about this hotel was Mother's design. When I tried to argue about something, Robert sided with her. She was pulling the strings all along. She placed him in that position." He sighed. "I didn't realize what their plan was until later. It wasn't until after Mother died that I learned she had forged my signature on a lot of documents."

He looked his father in the eye, something he didn't do often. "I didn't know she had used my signature to sign over the hotel to him until you called. That was her doing." *It was another betrayal at the hands of someone who was supposed to love him,* he thought. At twenty-eight, you would think he'd be used to it by now. But it never got any easier.

"Did you check out the work he was doing? Are you sure this hotel was built to code?"

Jerrod nodded his head. "Since he was planning on

claiming the hotel as his, he wouldn't do anything to make it fall down. If you look at the plans and everything that was done, you'll see that it's built not just to code, but it exceeds every code. The budget on this hotel alone topped all of the others you've built." His mother and cousin had plotted against him as well as against Mason. "Why did she hate you so much if it wasn't because you cheated on her?" There was no heat in his voice now.

Mason shook his head. "When we got married, her father gave me the two small motels he owned as a wedding present. I didn't want his motels but Belinda said turning them down would be a slap in the face. So I took them. I also paid for them. I gave him more than a fair price for it, but it wasn't enough. She twisted everything I did, and accused me of stealing them from her family." He shook his head. "She was a mean and spiteful woman. Nothing ever pleased her."

Mason took a good look at his son. There was still a lot of the little boy in there. He'd been betrayed by his mother, and maybe even his father. "I'm sorry, Son, for my part in all of this."

"Do you think there's a chance for us?" Jerrod's voice was small.

"I think we can try. It's going to take a lot of work on both of our parts. I'm willing if you are." He stood up and came around the big desk. Instead of offering his hand, he pulled his son in for a hug. He hadn't hugged any of his kids for far longer than he'd like to admit.

CHAPTER TWELVE

Cady had trouble concentrating on work for the rest of the day. Emotions roiled in her stomach each time the big doors swished open. Would Jerrod come back? Would he be waiting for her when she left work? She wanted to know what he'd told Darrell, but she said a prayer that Darrell wouldn't come to the library. She'd already caused enough gossip to last a lifetime.

Isabell and her book club ladies usually stayed in the library only long enough to trash their latest book choice before heading to the pub for happy hour. They claimed they went for the appetizers, but everyone knew they also enjoyed the half-priced well-drinks and wine. That day they stayed long past the start of happy hour before giving up their vigil in the hope that Jerrod would return for round two.

Finding the parking lot empty when she finally left the library at the end of the day, she breathed a sigh of relief. She'd give the deputy a call when she got home. She wanted to know what Jerrod had told him. She supposed having her life's secrets laid out for everyone to see was inevitable, but that didn't mean she was happy about it.

Calling him turned out to be unnecessary. Deputy Flanagan was leaning against a big pickup parked in front of her house when she pulled into the driveway. Since he was still in uniform she assumed he'd just gotten off work. Before she could gather her purse and book bag, Darrell opened her door for her. "Hi. How was the rest of your day?" He chuckled softly.

"About like you'd expect." She shook her head. "The normally quiet library was buzzing with talk all afternoon. People come out of the woodwork when there is something juicy to see. I'm sure everyone in town has heard about what happened and a lot that didn't happen."

He nodded his head. "Mrs. Brewster is determined to be in the middle of everything that happens in town. She's called the department several times wanting to know what we did about 'that young man who attacked our dear Cady Townsend this morning'." Making air quotes around the words, he chuckled. When Cady groaned, he was quick to assure her that Isabell didn't find out anything. "She was disappointed each time she called. Our department might be small, but no one is stupid."

"Thank you for that." Isabell and her friends wouldn't be as generous. They would make sure the rest of the town knew once they discovered the truth. This wasn't the 1800's when illegitimate children were punished for their parent's mistakes, but some people would still look down on her. Isabell Brewster was one of them. She loved dishing out dirt on anyone and everyone, and the dirtier the better.

Drawing a steadying breath, she asked, "Can you tell me what Jerrod had to say?" She wasn't sure why butterflies were attacking her stomach. He already knew her family's dirty little secret. She hoped there weren't any secrets left to tell.

"He denied any knowledge of what happened to you. He said he wasn't in town when someone shot at you or when you were run off the road. I've talked to several of his friends and the bartender at the club in San Francisco where the men were. He wasn't in Tumbleweed or Arizona on either of those nights. That doesn't mean he didn't have a hand in what happened. We'll need to check his financials to make sure he didn't pay someone to do it for him."

"Did he say why he was here?" She wasn't sure what she expected Jerrod to say.

"He said he came to talk to his father about some family matters. As long as it doesn't pertain to the two incidents involving you, and it isn't against the law, it doesn't concern the sheriff's department. Or Mrs. Brewster," he added with a chuckle.

"Thank you." After her short encounter with Jerrod, she had been afraid he would delight in laying out the family's dirty laundry to anyone willing to listen. "Do you know if he left town?"

"He said he'll be staying in town for a few days. I'm not sure if he's staying at his father's hotel. I did warn him to stay away from the library as long as you were there. He knows we will be watching him."

It would be interesting to know how his meeting with his father turned out. She was sure it hadn't happened in public or the entire town would know about it already. It wouldn't surprise her if Isabell tracked him down to question him. That could prove interesting if she did. He seemed to have a short fuse.

Looking up at the tall deputy, she waited. It seemed like he had more to say. Clearing his throat, he said, "Do you have plans for dinner tonight?"

A happy smile lit up her face. "No plans at all." Her stomach fluttered. "Do you have a suggestion?" It had been a long time since she'd found a man interesting enough to flirt with.

"I suggest you have dinner with me," he flirted back.

"I would like that very much. Would you like to come in while I freshen up? I'll leave a note for my mom so she won't worry when I'm not home." Most twenty-one-year-olds don't live with their parents, but Tumbleweed is a small town. There aren't a lot of options on either housing or men.

She'd grown up with most of the single men in town. Dating any of them always felt like going out with your brother. Dating someone from a nearby town didn't necessarily work out either. Besides, the nearest town was forty miles away. It might not be a great distance in the grand scheme of things, but it did create problems in a relationship.

That was why she'd first agreed to go out with Robert. Thinking about him now caused a shudder to move down her spine. Where he was? Mr. Jarvis, Mason, she mentally corrected herself, it was time she thought of him that way, said he'd been fired. But was he still in Tumbleweed? What would he do next? Was he behind what had been happening?

Those thoughts moved through her mind with the speed of light and were dismissed just as quickly. She smiled at the handsome man in front of her. What Robert did next wasn't her problem. Mason had attorneys to handle him.

"Do you have a preference on where we eat?" Darrell asked as he helped her into the high cab of his truck a few minutes later. She was dressed casually in a pair of black jeans with a western-cut blouse and boots. It was standard dress in any western town.

"Anywhere is fine as long as it isn't the restaurant at the Jarvis House Hotel." Her lips curved upward. Running into Jerrod over dinner would definitely ruin her appetite.

"Mexican food all right then?" There was a hopeful note in his voice.

"My favorite."

They had just settled in at a table in the back of the restaurant when Darrell groaned softly. "Here comes trouble." He looked up with a tight smile. "Good evening, Mrs. Brewster." He didn't bother to stand up. That might give her the idea he was inviting her to join them.

"Good evening, Deputy." She nodded her head at him before turning to Cady. "I couldn't help myself when I saw you come in here. I've been so worried about you all day. I wasn't able to find out if that horrible man was in jail." She sent Darrell a fierce frown.

"Thank you for checking on me, Isabell. I'm fine." She didn't say anything else hoping she would take the hint and leave. But hints didn't work on Isabell.

"Well, I'm so glad to see that you're okay. That man seemed so angry. Did you know him?"

"No, Ma'am."

"But you must know him. You wouldn't go into a room alone with a stranger, would you?" She looked positively gleeful at the prospect of forcing Cady to reveal some juicy gossip.

"The library is supposed to be a quiet place to read or study. I didn't want to disturb anyone."

"What did he want?" Isabell wasn't going to give up.

"We didn't have a chance to discuss what he wanted."

"But you must have." She was interrupted when the waiter stepped around her to place water, chips, and salsa on the table.

"Are you ready to order?" Juan had his order pad ready.

"Yes, I think we're ready," Darrell said. "If you'll excuse us, Mrs. Brewster?" One rust-colored eyebrow arched up slightly.

"Harrumph," she huffed. Turning on her heel, she marched out of the restaurant. They were highly mistaken if they thought they got the best of her. Pulling her phone out of her purse, she called for reinforcements.

Cady giggled when several people applauded Darrell's action and his face got pink beneath his deep tan. "I've never seen anyone get the best of Isabell before. She's going to be gunning for you now."

"She can say whatever she wants about me. It isn't going to affect me in the slightest." Looking up at Juan, he smiled his thanks. "Um, maybe we do need a couple of minutes to look at the menu."

"I know what I want," Cady said, looking at Juan. "I'll take my usual."

"Sure thing, Cady." He waited for Darrell to glance at the menu.

"I'll have the number three dinner." They each handed him their menus. "I take it you eat here a lot. What is your usual?"

"My girlfriends and I come here about once a week. We each have our favorites and seldom order something else. I always order a deep-fried bean burro enchilada style. It's almost big enough to share, but I enjoy the leftovers."

"That's good to know. I'll have to try that sometime." For several minutes silence enveloped them. Cady's mind was filled with the possibilities this evening might present. It had been a while since she'd met someone who consumed her thoughts the way the deputy did.

"Um, tell me about yourself," Darrell interrupted her thoughts. "Have you lived in Tumbleweed all your life?"

Cady nodded, her hair falling over the side of her face. Pushing it behind her ear, she answered. "Born and raised. Mom's parents had a cabin several miles from here and they used to come here on vacation when she was small. When it got too much for them to take care of, they sold it. But Mom never forgot the fun she had every summer. Her parents were both teachers so they were able to spend the entire summer here." Realizing she was rambling, she closed her lips.

Taking a breath, she smiled at him. "Sorry" She shrugged her shoulders. "You wanted to know about me, but probably not all in one breath."

"Oh, I'm sure there's a lot more to learn about you." His smile produced twin dimples in his cheeks to match the cleft in his chin. "We can take it slow. I'll enjoy learning all about you."

Feeling her face heat up, she was grateful when Juan placed steaming plates in front of them.

When Juan added a second plate in front of Darrell, his eyes got large. "I guess I didn't read the menu close enough. That's enough food to feed a family of four." Juan chuckled as he walked away.

"Take my word for it. The leftovers are just as good the next day."

"Glad to hear it because I'll never be able to finish all of this in one sitting. I see now why you order off the Ala Carte menu."

Long after they finished eating, they stayed at the table. Cady couldn't recall ever enjoying someone's company as much as she did his. "You know I grew up here in Tumbleweed. Where did you call home before joining the sheriff's department?"

"The longest we were in one place was four years. My dad was career Navy so we moved around a lot. I went to three different high schools. I vowed I would never do that to my kids when I got married. So when I got out of the Marines I made sure I wouldn't be moving from one place to the next every few years. Tumbleweed seems like a nice place to raise a family." His intense gaze caused a warm blush to creep over Cady's face.

Leaving the restaurant, it felt natural for him to take her hand in his much bigger one as they walked down the sidewalk. Looking up at the stars, Cady sighed with contentment. If this night never ended, she would be happy.

"I take it you enjoy hiking through the forest," Darrell said after several minutes. The silence was comfortable, but he still wanted to know about her.

"I did until the other night," she said with a small laugh. "Until you catch whoever did that, I won't be doing any hiking at night. Maybe even during the day," she added with a small shudder.

He nodded his head in agreement. "It would be a good idea to hold off until we catch him. I wish I could say we were closing in on a suspect, but we aren't. There just aren't many clues to follow. The forest tends to erase things left behind. Except for trash," he added. "People think nothing of leaving

113

their trash behind for someone else to pick up. This time it would have been nice if he'd left something besides the shell casings."

"I doubt he was in the forest for very long." They were both assuming the assailant was a man. It could just as easily be a woman though. She didn't know anyone that hated her enough to want her dead except Jerrod Jarvis and his sister. With a sigh, she pushed that thought aside. "I didn't even know I was going to be in the forest until I ended up there."

Wanting to change the subject, she asked, "What else did Jerrod say when you took him to the station?"

"Not much. He said he came to talk to his father about a family matter. I haven't had a chance to speak with Mr. Jarvis yet. When I asked why he went to see you, he repeated himself. It's a family matter. When I pressed him about what he was doing at the library, he refused to say. He didn't harm you or threaten you so I couldn't hold him any longer. What did he say to you?"

She sighed. "He said he wanted to meet his half-sister and see what a gold digger looked like. Apparently, he's afraid I'm going to claim some part of his inheritance." She shook her head. "I don't have any claim on anything belonging to Mason Jarvis, nor do I want to."

"I'm sure Mr. Jarvis will have something to say about that. Has he always known about you?"

She nodded her head. "Yes, he's known about me all along. I was the one left in the dark." Resentment reared its ugly head again. When she would have pulled her hand from his, his grip tightened. He wasn't ready to break the connection between them. It had nothing to do with either of the Jarvis men. He simply enjoyed holding her hand.

"Growing up without a father never bothered me," she finally said. "It never occurred to me to ask about him. My best friend's dad had died in a car accident when we were five or six." She shrugged. "Kids tend to simplify things. I thought my dad was dead like hers was. Mom never said anything. Until he showed up, that is." She sighed.

Her thoughts slipped back to the night when her world turned upside down. "After Mom dropped that bombshell on me, I stormed out of the house. I drove around for a long time and I ended up at my best friend's apartment. I spent the night there. I didn't want to go home. I knew eventually I would have to let Mom explain, but not right then. She was waiting for me on Friday when I got home from work." Should she tell him everything she'd learned? It was eventually going to come out.

Giving a mental shrug, she continued. "She'd met Mason Jarvis right after she got out of college and they fell in love. Of course, he was married and had a son and daughter." Without realizing it, her tone had turned bitter again.

"You don't have to tell me this if you'd rather not."

She lifted her shoulders, letting them drop. "I shouldn't let it bother me, but it does. Not that they weren't married to each other when I was born, but that she withheld this from me all my life. Why wouldn't she tell me?" Unshed tears sparkled in her dark eyes when she looked up at him. "That's what hurts the most. Other than Blair, Mom was my best friend while I was growing up. I always thought we could tell each other anything. Apparently not."

"Did she tell you the circumstances?"

She nodded. "He hired her to tutor his older kids. She said they were out of control and his wife was a witch. But isn't that sort of thing men tell their mistresses. 'My wife doesn't understand me.' I'm not sure if it's true." She sighed. "Anyway, after airing her dirty laundry, I needed time to sort through what she'd said. That's when I went for a walk. I never planned on ending up in the forest. The rest, as they say, is history."

"So whoever shot at you had to have been following you. Otherwise, they wouldn't have known you would be in the forest at that particular time." The thought that someone was following her caused Cady's heart to skip a beat. "Can you think of anyone who would want to do this?" He'd asked her that before. She still couldn't come up with a clear answer.

"The only people I've had trouble with recently are Robert Gates, I mean, Gaston, Jerrod Jarvis, and his father." She shrugged. "Of course, Isabell Brewster is none too happy with me at the moment either." She laughed. She couldn't see the older woman trekking through the forest to shoot her.

"I haven't been able to locate Robert Gaston," Darrell said. "He's never in his apartment when I stop by. His cell phone has been disconnected as well. Until I'm able to have a chat with him, please be extra careful." He placed his lips lightly against her.

It was late when he brought her home. The limo wasn't sitting in front of the house, but a strange car was parked behind her car. Maybe Mason had decided not to advertise his presence at Olivia's house and had rented a regular car after all. Going in now meant she would have to talk to him. She didn't want that either.

"You think I could climb that tree and get in my bedroom that way?" She looked up at Darrell. For a long moment, she was lost in his green eyes.

"Climbing the tree might not be a good idea," he chuckled. "I'd hate for your mom to think someone was breaking in and call the department. That could get a little embarrassing." He lowered his head, capturing her lips again. His tongue ran along the seam of her lips, begging entry.

They were both breathing heavily several minutes later when he lifted his head. "I've been thinking of doing that since that night you walked out of the forest and almost fell into my arms." He didn't give her a chance to say anything as

116

he kissed her again. Several kisses later he opened his door and stepped out. He needed to slow things down. The cool air felt good on his overheated skin.

Since she was out of practice climbing the tree, she led him around to the back door instead. If she was quiet, she might be able to sneak up the back stairs without her mom hearing her. "Thank you for dinner and for listening to me ramble on," she whispered. "I hope you don't think less of me for what happened."

"What your folks did or didn't do is no reflection on you. Everyone has something in their past they would rather others don't find out." He placed nibbling kisses from her ear to her jaw before claiming her lips again in a long kiss. "You are who you are because of the way your mom raised you. I think she did a great job. I'll see you tomorrow." He was whistling softly as he walked back to his truck.

CHAPTER THIRTEEN

Tiptoeing up the back stairs, Cady made it to her room without disturbing her mom and Mason. She didn't want to ruin the perfect evening she'd spent with Darrell by talking about Jerrod's visit to the library that morning. It looked like Mason was going to be a permanent fixture in her mom's life. That meant in hers as well. She wasn't sure how she felt about that. Hopefully, Jerrod would go back to wherever he was from and stay there

Pushing those thoughts out of her mind, she flopped down on her bed. Remembering the kisses she'd shared with Darrell, her skin got warm. Of all the surprises she'd had recently, he was the most welcome surprise in her life. She fell asleep with a happy smile on her face.

Arriving at the library the next morning, she was surprised to find Henry packing up his meager belongings. "What's going on, Henry?"

"Think maybe it's time for me to be moving on. I heard you had another close call over the weekend. Something bad is going on in this town." He kept his head down as he stuffed what remained of his belongings into his knapsack. He hadn't been around the day before. But that wasn't unusual. He moved around so he didn't make a nuisance of himself. But he'd never packed up his few belongings before.

"What does that have to do with you?" She was confused.

"Folks are always looking for people to blame when bad things keep happening. Don't want them thinking I'm the cause of all your trouble."

"No one would think that." He'd never been anything but nice to her. She hoped he felt the same way about his encounters with her. "I know you wouldn't hurt me."

"Maybe so, but others think bad of anyone living behind a

dumpster. You're one of the good ones, that's for sure, Miss Cady. There's others that aren't so nice. That there Mrs. Brewster tries to run me off every time she sees me. She threatened to have me arrested if I didn't move. She's not a nice lady like you."

Cady silently agreed with him. "She had no right threatening you like that, and I'm sorry. I'll miss you when you're gone. I've enjoyed visiting with you in the mornings. Where are you going?"

"Don't rightly know yet, but don't worry none about me. Before I go though, I could use a bottle of water to take with me." He looked at her hopefully.

"I can do that for you. There's bottled water in the workroom. I'll bring you out some right away. I also brought you coffee and a donut." She handed him the to-go cup and the small bag with his favorite donut.

"Thank you kindly, Miss Cady. That's what I mean. You're always kind to me."

What had Isabell said to him? Why would she try to run him off? He wasn't hurting anyone. She knew a lot of homeless people cared little about the mess they made and didn't bother cleaning up when they moved on. There had been a small encampment of homeless in the alley behind a local restaurant recently. The mess they'd left in the alley was awful. Had Isabell managed to have them run out of town?

Mentally ill people were a large part of the homeless population in recent years. They were mostly harmless, but if they were off their meds the slightest thing could set them off. She didn't know what the solution was. She felt sorry for those who were homeless through no fault of their own. It was the ones who chose to live on the street because they didn't want to work that she had no pity for.

Before settling in at her desk, she got several bottles of water out of the workroom and hurried back outside. The alley was empty. Henry's knapsack and bedroll were gone. Why didn't he wait for the water she'd promised him? Had someone run him off before she could do that? Not even Isabell worked that fast. Looking up and down the alley, it was empty. Henry was simply gone.

Placing the bottles on the ground beside the dumpster, she went back inside. If Henry returned, he could get his water. If not, maybe some other soul could have it.

That was the way of the homeless. They moved on when the spirit moved them. She didn't know Henry's story, but she assumed it was like so many others. A job lost, followed closely by losing their home. Soon all hope was gone and they drifted along. He seemed to enjoy the life of a vagabond. Asking God to keep him safe was all she could do for him now.

Memories of the night before quickly consumed her thoughts. The evening hadn't been anything special, but it had been very special. Darrell had said he'd call her today. She checked her phone, to make sure it was on and had plenty of power. She didn't want to miss his call.

Cady groaned when she saw who was waiting for the door to be unlocked a short time later. The Ladies Book Club wasn't supposed to meet until Friday and she'd never known Eleanor Davis to come to the library at any other time. She was sure Eleanor only attended the meetings because of the visit to the pub after the meeting.

"Good morning, Eleanor." The older woman appeared nervous as she stood in front of Cady's desk. "You're out and about early this morning. How are you?"

"Oh, um, I'm fine." Whatever she had on her mind was making her more nervous with each passing second. "How are you?" She asked belatedly. She began wringing her hands.

"I'm fine, Eleanor. Are you sure you're all right?" She frowned at the older woman. "Is there something I can help you with?"

"Oh, no, I mean yes, I'm fine." Shuffling her feet, she looked at her hands as if expecting to find some answers there. But maybe there were. "Um, ah, I saw you last night with that handsome new deputy. He sure is a good-looking boy."

"That he is, but I'm not sure he would appreciate being called a boy." Cady tried to hide the smile tugging at her lips. The woman was here on a mission for Isabell, but she wasn't doing a very good job.

"Of course." Eleanor's face turned red. She wasn't very good at prying into other people's lives. "I didn't mean anything by that." She shifted from one foot to the other like she needed to use the restroom. Her mom had always called that the 'potty dance' when Cady was growing up.

"Um, ah," she started again. "We... ah... me I mean I," she was stammering now. Taking several gulps of air, she tried again. "I thought you were seeing that nice manager at the new hotel in town. You know, the one that Mr. Jarvis owns." She glanced at her hand again. The gesture was reminiscent of the way students looked for the answers they'd written on their palms before taking a test. Cady was sure she saw blue ink on her hand.

She covered her laugh with a cough. Isabell's desire to find out what Mason's relationship was to Olivia and Cady was making her desperate. She felt sorry for Eleanor, but not so sorry she was going to tell her anything.

After studying her hand for several seconds, Eleanor looked at Cady again. "We... I mean I haven't seen him around lately. Did he leave town? It must have been sudden." She kept forgetting to make it sound like she wanted to know instead of Isabell.

Cady shrugged her shoulders, trying to remain calm. She no longer saw any humor in this. Isabell had stepped over the line this time. What business was it of hers anyway? "I'm afraid Isabell will have to ask him that question, not me."

Eleanor's face turned red at being caught. "Oh." She blinked several times unsure where to go from there. She looked at her hand again, but apparently, it wasn't much help. "But you were dating him," she insisted.

"And now I'm not," Cady stated. She shrugged again but didn't offer any other information.

"Um, we... I heard that the owner of the hotel is staying in town. His son is here as well."

"Is that so?" One dark brow arched upward. How much longer would this go on before her temper reached the boiling point? If Isabell was there now, she'd tell the woman what she thought of her prying into everyone's business.

"Well, yes it is." Eleanor was confused now. "Isabell was right here when he came in. She said you went into the workroom with him. When he came out, that handsome deputy took him away."

It hadn't taken long for Isabell to ferret out the information that Jerrod was Mason's son. How long before she found out that Cady was his daughter? She sighed. A secret only remained a secret when only one person knew it. There were far too many people that knew the truth for it to remain a secret for long.

"I guess you need to talk to Isabell then. I have nothing to say. Now, if you'll excuse me, I have work that needs to be done." She pushed her chair back and stood up. Eleanor was still standing there with a confused expression on her face as Cady walked away. She was easily led about by Isabell, and again Cady felt sorry for her. *Almost,* she silently added.

For the remainder of the day, Cady expected Isabell to show up demanding answers to her questions. Of course, her curiosity wasn't going to be satisfied. Why did gossips feel that they had the right to know everything about everybody?

All she needed now was for Mason's daughter, his other

daughter, to show up. She sighed. If the Jarvis' would leave town, things might go back to normal. But something told her that wasn't going to happen. Without his wife's threats holding him back, Mason seemed determined to win both Olivia and Cady over. She was still trying to figure out how she felt about that. Did she want to get to know him, and by extension, her half-siblings?

Mason had admitted Jerrod and Melanie weren't very nice. If the way Jerrod had acted the other day was any indication, he was right. She still didn't know what Jerrod had hoped to gain by coming here and confronting her. He obviously thought she was after his dad's money. How could she prove that wasn't the case? She'd be just as happy if he had stayed away for the rest of her life.

Eleanor had asked one legitimate question. Where was Robert? She hadn't heard from him since the morning after her birthday. Mason said he'd fired the man, so where was he? Had he left town? If he really believed he owned the hotel in Tumbleweed, would he take Mason to court? He'd claimed to have paperwork proving Mason had cheated his grandfather. Of course, Mason said he had paperwork saying he hadn't. Her head was spinning with all the unanswered questions.

CHAPTER FOURTEEN

Cady had been half expecting Isabell to put in an appearance after Eleanor had failed to garner the information she was looking for. She wasn't disappointed. "Good afternoon, Isabell. Is there something I can help you with?"

"It has come to my attention that you have allowed a homeless man to take up residence behind this building. I would like to know why. This is the property of the town, not your private residence." This wasn't the topic foremost on her mind, but she'd start slow.

"Henry wasn't hurting anything," Cady stated quietly hoping Isabell would take the hint. She should have known better. "He picked up trash that other people left behind. He made sure no one broke into the library when it was closed. You had no right threatening him."

"People of his ilk don't belong around the good people of this town." She'd never known Isabell to be so uppity. She was a gossip to be sure and could be nasty when embellishing her tales, but Cady never thought she was mean at heart.

"Then again, I'm not sure you and your mother belong here either." Her nose turned up as though she'd gotten a whiff of something rotten.

"What is that supposed to mean?" A muscle bunched in Cady's jaw. She had a pretty fair idea where this was going.

"It means I know all about your mother and that high and mighty Mr. Jarvis. You're the product of an illicit love affair." She stopped short of calling Cady a bastard. Her voice got higher on each word.

"Isabell, I'm going to have to ask you to keep your voice down. People are trying to concentrate here."

"Don't tell me what to do, young lady," the older woman snipped. "Folks have the right to know the kind of people hired to take care of other… um people." She was confusing herself.

"Who told you this?" Heads were popping up all over the library as they took notice of this conversation.

"A lady never divulges where she gets her information," Isabell stated haughtily. "But I assure you I have it on good faith. I'm not sure you and Olivia are the type of folks this town wants teaching our children."

"I suppose you'd rather they learn from gossip whispered about behind closed doors," Cady said. "I've lived in this town my entire life. I've never been in trouble. My mother has lived here since before I was born. Neither of us has done anything to harm anyone. I'm sure you've heard the adage 'People who live in glass houses shouldn't throw stones.' You might want to take a good look at your own actions before you start making accusations toward others. Everyone in this town has been on the brunt end of your gossip for years." She stared at the older woman, daring her to say anything more.

Isabell's face turned an angry shade of purple. Cady thought she was going to have a stroke or heart attack. Instead, she turned and stomped out without another word to Cady.

The cat is out of the bag now, Cady thought. Her stomach was in knots and for a minute she thought she was going to throw up. It wouldn't be long before this episode was all over town. How far would Isabell stretch the truth in an effort to make herself look good and Cady and Olivia look like scarlet ladies of the night? She refused to let Isabell ruin her life. She was still the same person she'd been two weeks ago.

Who had told Isabell? It was certain Mason hadn't said anything to her. That still left a lot of people who knew the circumstances of her birth. The two most likely though were Jerrod and Robert. She hadn't seen Robert since the day after her birthday. Where was he? Mason didn't have a good relationship with his son. Would Jerrod jeopardize any possibility of forging a bond with his dad by doing this? She couldn't answer that question.

"Cady? Are you all right?" Startled, Cady looked up at Martha, her assistant. "Don't pay any attention to Isabell. No one is going to think less of you for something your mother did. Olivia is a good person. What happened in the past shouldn't make any difference." It was obvious everyone had heard what Isabell said.

"I'm fine, Martha." Cady tried to collect her composure.

"Was she upset because Henry has been staying behind the dumpster? He wouldn't hurt a fly," she said indignantly. "She's more dangerous with all of her lies than Henry is."

"I know, but she won't have to worry about him any longer. He left this morning."

"What? Why? You don't have to answer that. It's because of Isabell. That woman is a real b... I mean witch." Martha's face turned red. "She's always sticking her nose in where it doesn't belong." She was mumbling as she walked away.

Shaking her head, Cady sigh. It wouldn't be long before Isabell's lies were all over town. But they weren't exactly lies. Her mom did have an affair with a married man. She was illegitimate. None of that should matter, but people were unpredictable. She couldn't even guess what the school board would do about Olivia's job. What would the town council have to say about her?

There was nothing to be done about any of this now. She did intend on talking to her half-brother. If he's the one that told Isabell, she was going to... She didn't know what she was going to do. There was nothing she could do. *You can't unring a bell*, she thought

Time seemed to stand still for the remainder of the afternoon. Each time she looked at the clock, only minutes had passed. She was unable to concentrate on work. Her imagination was spinning with possibilities of what Isabell was telling people.

Darrell was waiting when Cady left the library that evening. He was still on duty, but he needed to see her. Like most everyone else in town, he'd heard what Isabell was saying. The woman needed to be stopped, but how do you stop a gossip? Raising a fuss would only place more credence on what she was saying.

"Are you okay?" A worried frown drew his rust-colored brows into a V over his eyes. He wanted to take her into his arms but he knew better. People were already talking about Cady and her mom. He didn't want to add fuel to an already burning fire.

"I will be." She nodded her head, brushing her dark hair away from her face. "I suppose you heard about what happened today." It was a statement, not a question.

"Yes, I wish there was some way I could stop her. Unfortunately gossip isn't against the law."

Cady sighed. "There's nothing you or anyone else can do. I don't know exactly all that she's saying, but she doesn't even have to embellish the truth to get people's attention. She made sure everyone in the library heard her. By now, there's probably very little truth to what is being said though."

She ran both hands through her hair in frustration. "All she had to do was put a little bit of truth out there and let human nature take it from there. It's what Isabell always does. This way she can deny having any part in ruining our reputation."

"Why would she do this?" He was angry for Cady. He wanted to protect her.

Cady shrugged. "It's just the way she operates."

"Do you know who told her?"

"No, but I can guess. There aren't that many people who know Mason is my birth father. Obviously, Mom's never told anyone since she didn't even tell me." The bitterness she'd first felt when she learned the truth was still there. She drew a deep breath, letting it out slowly. "Other than Isabell, no one else would enjoy telling everyone about what happened between my mom and Mason Jarvis. At least I don't think I have any enemies besides Jerrod Jarvis and Robert Gates, I mean Gaston."

Darrell shook his head. "It wasn't Jerrod. I've already talked to him. Neither he nor his dad knew anything about what's being said until I went to question him. They've been together all day." He sighed.

"What was Jerrod doing with his dad?" A confused frown creased her forehead. "I thought they would be barely speaking after he visited the library yesterday."

Darrell shrugged. "It looked like they were trying to repair their relationship. But Mr. Jarvis was ready to strangle someone, his son included, when I told them about what's going on. I know gossip isn't within the wheelhouse of the sheriff's department, but you're within my wheelhouse." He stroked one finger down the side of Cady's face. "Unless he saw Mrs. Brewster before he went to see his dad, it wasn't Jerrod."

"I guess that leaves Robert," Cady sighed. "I don't know if he's still in town. I'm not exactly sure how he would benefit by doing this though."

"I haven't seen him around town, but I haven't been looking for him either. You can bet I'll be looking for him now." His voice was fierce.

Cady had bared her soul at dinner. She still couldn't believe how easy he was to talk to. It hadn't appeared like it changed his opinion of her or her mom. Being seen with her after the truth was out didn't seem to bother him either.

"What are you doing later tonight?" His eyebrows arched up slightly. "I don't get off work until late, but I'd like to see you, even for a few minutes."

"Nothing. I'm all yours." Her face got hot when she

realized the implications of her words. "I mean…"

"I like your answer no matter what you mean. I'll call when I get off work." Leaning down the few inches separating them, he placed a light kiss on her lips. If people wanted to put a bad spin on the kiss, he didn't care. They weren't doing anything wrong.

Turning the corner onto her street, Cady sighed. Mason Jarvis's rental car was parked in front of the house. Weren't the flapping lips bad enough without him adding to the talk? Darrell said Jerrod had been with his father all day. He couldn't be the one that told Isabell about Cady's parentage. She still didn't want to sit around the dinner table with either of them. She was still having trouble coming to grips with all that she'd learned in the past weeks.

She stopped just inside the kitchen staring at the cozy scene. Olivia was making dinner as she did most nights when she got home before Cady. Mason was setting the kitchen table. Jerrod was holding a wine glass. It looked like any normal 'family' dinner. But they were far from a normal family.

"Hi, Honey. Come on in. No one is going to bite you." Olivia smiled at her. Despite the gossip about them making its way through town, she seemed unconcerned.

"Care for a glass of wine?" Jerrod held up his glass in invitation. There was a full bottle on the table beside him. His face was flushed and she wondered how much he'd already had. His mother was an alcoholic and his sister wasn't far behind if she wasn't a full-fledged alcoholic by now. Did that mean he was also?

"No thank you. I'm not in the mood. I just came home to change clothes." Her tone was stilted, her gaze cool. It hadn't been that long since he'd stormed into the library ready to burn the place down with her in it.

She turned to Mason. "I know you're aware of what's

129

being said about us. I don't know how you can sit there like nothing is wrong in our world."

"Cady Elizabeth Townsend, that's enough." Olivia's voice was sharp. "There is no call for you to be rude."

"No, Olivia, it's all right. She has every right to be upset with all of us. I know I went about things the wrong way a long time ago and I've hurt all of my children."

"Don't include me in with them. I was fine until a week ago. I wasn't the topic of dinner conversation all over town, and my name wasn't being dragged through the mud." She turned to look at her mother. "I'm sorry if this hurts you, but I've had quite enough for one day. I'm going up to my room to change clothes. Then I'm going out."

"Where are you going? After everything that's happened lately, you can't go alone."

She glared at Mason. "You don't have the right to tell me what I can and can't do. You gave up that right a long time ago." Without another word, she stormed up the stairs. Tears burned the back of her eyes, but she refused to let them fall. Darrell said it would be after eight when he got off work. She had her phone with her. She wasn't sitting around here playing nice with the people that have hurt her recently.

Olivia followed her up the stairs. "Honey, I'm sorry for how I've handled things. I hope you can eventually forgive me, forgive all of us. I thought I was doing the right thing by not saying anything about Mason."

"What about right now? What's with this cozy family dinner thing going on? I'm happy that things are working out for you. But you can't expect me to join in the fun, not after today."

Olivia nodded. "All right. I can understand. But you don't have to be rude."

"Rude?" Cady almost screeched. "Do you have any idea how I felt when Isabell was dishing out the dirt on us? There were a lot of people in the library at the time. That's probably why she chose that time to come in. She was angry that I didn't answer Eleanor's questions first thing this morning. So, don't tell me not to be rude. I've had rude shoved in my face today."

"I'm sorry about that, but if you run away and hide you're letting her win."

"Tonight, I need to let her win. You didn't see the looks on the faces of those people in the library when she was telling all of our dirty secrets."

"They aren't your secrets and they aren't dirty. You aren't to blame for what happened between Mason and me, and it isn't anyone else's business."

"Well, Isabell made it their business. You weren't there when Jerrod came into the library either. He wasn't exactly Mr. Congeniality. Isabell conveniently happened to be there for that as well."

"Jerrod has apologized to me for his recent actions and he would like the chance to tell you he's sorry as well."

"Oh, if all it takes to make amends is to say you're sorry, then I'm sorry for walking out tonight." Her tone was sarcastic. "Because that's exactly what I'm doing."

"Cady, please." Olivia reached out to touch her daughter but stopped when Cady pulled away from her.

"Mom, don't you care what Isabell is saying about us? The people in this town are our friends. Or I thought they were. They're thinking the worst about you, about me."

"Then they aren't our friends," Olivia stated simply.

"But we still have to live here. Isabell is threatening to go to the school board and town council to have us fired. Doesn't that matter to you?"

"Of course it does, but she can't do that. She has no say in what the school board or town council does. If they're swayed by gossip and by what I did more than twenty-one years

131

ago…" She lifted her shoulders in a shrug. "I can't stop them. As Jesus said, 'Let him who is without sin, throw the first stone.' You have done nothing wrong. This isn't the 1800's where illegitimate children are punished for what their parents did." She echoed Cady's own earlier thoughts.

Cady flinched at those words. She needed to get tougher skin because it won't be long before she's called a lot worse than illegitimate.

Cady continued to change into a pair of jeans. "At least tell me where you're going," Olivia said. "Someone has tried to harm you twice. You shouldn't be out alone."

"I won't be alone. The entire town will be watching, waiting for me to screw up. If someone tries to kill me, there will be plenty of witnesses. There might even be one or two willing to step in and help me." She was being melodramatic, but she couldn't help it.

"I've done a lot of things wrong in regards to what happened between Mason and me. That can't be changed. But no one is going to blame you."

Cady gave her a skeptical look but didn't argue. Taking out her gym bag, she put in clothes for the next day. "Are you running away like you did when you were a little girl and got upset with me?" Olivia couldn't believe how this had gotten blown all out of proportion. Isabell needed to pay for what she was doing.

"Yes, Mom, I'm running away. I'll talk to you later." Tears were streaming down her face as she sailed down the stairs. She didn't stop when she reached the kitchen. She didn't want to see Mason or Jerrod.

Two blocks away, she pulled to the side of the road. She needed to stop crying or stop driving. She couldn't do both without having an accident. She felt there were few people she could count on not to judge her. She knew right where she was going.

"Are you okay?" Blair didn't bother saying hi when she answered the phone. "I can't believe what Isabell is doing."

"Can I spend the night at your place? I can't be home right now."

"You know you can."

Grateful for the safe haven, Cady pulled back onto the road. What would she tell Darrell when he called? He already knew about the skeletons in her family closet and didn't hold it against her. She didn't care how late it was when he called, she wanted to see him.

Blair had a glass of wine waiting for her when she opened the door. Giving her a quick hug, she placed the glass in her hand. "Someone needs to put a muzzle on Isabell."

"I'd love to be the one to do it, but it's too late. The cat's out of the bag. There's no taking it back now." She felt wrung out and left to dry.

It was closer to nine than eight when Darrell finally called. She was beginning to wonder if all the talk had gotten to him as well. "Are you okay? How did it go when you got home?"

"It didn't," she sighed. "I'm afraid I blew it. Mason and Jerrod were both there."

"Both?" That surprised him. It sounded like Jerrod had done a one-eighty turn since the day he'd met him.

"Yeah. He apologized so Mom's fine. I'm not quite so forgiving. I'm staying at Blair's apartment tonight. Can you stop by for a few minutes? I know you need to get some rest, but…"

"You don't have to say anymore. Tell me where she lives, I'll be there." He was still in his uniform when he arrived a few minutes later. Pulling her close, he placed a kiss on top of her head. "I've heard a lot of negative things about Isabell today. Not everyone is buying into what she's saying."

"Unless she's gone beyond what she said at the library, she's only telling the truth."

133

"That will be a first for her," Blair said as she stepped into the living room. She smiled at Darrell. "Hi, I'm Blair Ratcliff." She held out her hand.

He accepted her hand without releasing Cady. "From everything I've heard about Mrs. Brewster, the woman isn't very nice." He looked down at Cady. "Someday her gossip is going to get her in trouble."

He only stayed long enough to make sure Cady was all right. It had been a long day and a rough one for her. "Try to get some sleep. Things will look better in the morning." He placed a soft kiss on her lips and left. Those words couldn't be more wrong.

CHAPTER FIFTEEN

When her phone rang before the sun was even up, she expected it was her mom. Tempted to ignore it, she checked caller ID instead. "Good morning," she purred softly. "What…"

"Cady, I wanted to be the one to tell you before the gossips got ahold of it." Darrell cut her off. "Isabell Brewster is dead. Her body was found in the dumpster behind the Jarvis House Hotel early this morning."

Cady gasped, sitting up so fast her head began to spin. "What? How? Who?" She couldn't form a complete sentence.

"I don't have any answers. I probably shouldn't even be telling you."

"Am I a suspect? Don't answer that. Of course, I am. So is Mom. Oh, my gosh, so are Mason and Jerrod." She pushed her hair away from her face. "What should I do?"

"Go to work like you would any other day. Don't say anything to anyone about what happened yesterday with her. I don't know when I'll be able to call you. Just remember one thing." He paused. "I'm falling in love with you. We'll get this cleared up. Talk to you soon." The line went dead.

"He's falling in love with me," she whispered, unable to believe that or anything he'd said. It seemed unreal.

"Who's falling in love with you?" Blair came out of her bedroom rubbing sleep from her eyes. "Who called this early in the morning?"

"It was Darrell."

"Oh, he's falling in love with you." She frowned. "I thought that would make you happy." She tilted her head to one side letting her hair fall into her face. "What's going on?"

"I am happy about that. But…" He said not to talk about this. She had to tell Blair. A nurse at the community hospital,

135

she would hear all about it when she got to work. "Isabell is dead." Her voice was soft as though saying the words out loud would make it true.

Blair plopped down in the chair. "What? How?"

"I don't know, but after yesterday I'm a suspect. So are Mom, Mason, and Jerrod. I have to call her." Before she could reach for her phone, it rang. "It's Mom."

"Cady, are you all right? Have you heard about Isabell? Where are you? I'm so sorry about last night." Her words tumbled out before Cady could say anything.

"I'm fine, Mom. I'm sorry about last night, too. I was being a brat. Darrell called to tell me about..." She couldn't bring herself to say the words again. "We're all suspects."

"I know," Olivia sighed. How had things gotten so messed up? It seemed like fate was against her and Mason ever being together. "Where are you, honey?"

"At Blair's."

Olivia gave a small chuckle. "I should have known. The two of you have always been closer than a lot of sisters. Are you sure we're all right? I should have realized how everything was going to affect you. I just wanted things to be good for all of us. Jerrod truly seems to want to make amends. He and Mason still have a lot to work out between them, but at least he's trying."

"We're fine, Mom. I'll be home tonight. Unless I'm in jail, that is." Her stomach twisted at the possibility.

Was Jerrod sincere about working things out with his dad? After hating him for most of his life, how could he change overnight? She pushed those thoughts aside. There were more important matters to consider. Who had killed Isabell and why? Would any of them be able to prove they hadn't killed her?

As head librarian, she was her own boss. But she still answered to the town council. Mayor Bailey was waiting at the door when she unlocked it. "I suppose you've heard about

Isabell."

She nodded her head. She would have to be living under a rock not to have heard. The other employees had all stopped to get her take on Isabell's murder. Darrell said not to talk about what happened the day before, so she'd let the mayor do the talking.

"I know you and your mom had nothing to do with this. But I don't know about Mr. Jarvis or his son. The sheriff needs to sort this out. Isabell has been skating on thin ice many times over the years. Her gossiping finally caught up with her." He shook his head. "I came here to tell you that the council and I are behind you."

"Thank you, Mayor Bailey. I appreciate that. I know Mom will also."

"Okay." He wasn't sure what else to say. "Um, I'll see you later. Keep your head down and this will all go away." Cady thought this was only the tip of the iceberg. Something a lot bigger than Isabell's murder was going on.

~~~

This was the last day of school before the summer break. Olivia had three months for the gossip to die down before she had to face the students again. Hopefully, by that time, the police would have captured Isabell's killer. Until then, she would still have to face the people in town. Would this make people look at her and Cady differently?

The police didn't have much to say about how Isabell died or why she ended up in the dumpster behind the hotel when they came to question her first thing that morning. She knew they couldn't give out that kind of information, but their silence had everyone speculating about why she had been killed and by whom. The students were also understandably curious. Like everyone else, they had connected the gossip about Olivia with Isabell's murder.

Isabell was the source of all gossip in town. Her students

wanted to know whether that had anything to do with her death. Not saying anything about the murder made it look like she was hiding something. Still, she knew very little about what happened to Isabell.

"I don't know any more about what happened to Mrs. Brewster than anyone else," she told each class. "The sheriff's department is working to find her killer." When the questions turned personal, she shut them down. "I'm not going to answer any questions about what happened between Mr. Jarvis and me. That has nothing to do with the murder." But it probably did. Who would want to stop the gossip more than Cady, Mason, Jerrod, and her?

Mason had finally called her at lunch. A detective had been questioning him and Jerrod most of the morning. There were security cameras all around the hotel property. The one camera that would tell who the killer was had conveniently been disabled with a mixture of oatmeal and water to make it look like a bird had pooped on the lens. Whoever did this knew what they were doing and where the cameras were. They wanted to point a guilty finger at Mason and Jerrod.

It had been close to eleven when they left Olivia's. There had been no reason to check with security before going to their suite. The first Mason heard about the murder was when a security officer woke him at five-thirty. An employee had taken trash out to the dumpster and found her body.

"If this is what small towns are like," Jerrod groused over breakfast, "I'll take a big city any day."

"Small towns aren't immune to crime," Mason said with a shake of his head. "It just stands out more because there is less to report on."

"I'd still rather be in the city."

"How do you think you're going to run this hotel from San Francisco?" he asked mildly. A lopsided grin played around his lips.

"What do you mean?" Jerrod's eyes narrowed slightly. What was his dad telling him?

"This hotel still needs a manager. I can't stay here and run things along with everything else. Do you still want the job?"

Jerrod was speechless for several minutes. "Sure, I mean yes, I want the job."

"Even if it means living in a small town?" Mason joked.

"Even if." Jerrod nodded his head. There were still a lot of things to work out between them, but this was a start. He had to prove himself, and he was determined not to screw things up. The lies his mother had told to him and Melanie had always prevented them from being close. At least Mason claimed they were lies.

He gave a mental shrug. Only time would tell. Belinda was gone. If there was such a thing as Heaven and Hell, she was paying for everything she'd done to all of them.

~~~

The book club ladies marched into the library shortly after it opened. Standing in front of Cady's desk, there were varying expressions on their faces. "May I help you ladies?" She waited to see who would be the leader of the pack now that Isabell was gone.

"We want to know why Isabell was murdered." Eleanor's face was flushed.

"That's a question for the police, not me." She was surprised to find the normally meek Eleanor was the spokesperson. A few days ago, she'd barely been able to stutter out the questions Isabell had sent her to ask.

"The police won't tell us anything."

She shrugged. "I'm sorry, but I don't know any more than you do." Because she and Olivia were the target for Isabell's latest gossip campaign, the library was busier than normal. Everyone wanted to be close in case there was any breaking news on the topic of Isabell's murder. She kept her voice soft hoping Eleanor would do the same. There was already enough gossip and speculation floating around. She didn't want to add to it.

"We are all aware of what Isabell found out about you and your mother." Eleanor didn't bother to keep her voice down. She was doing a good imitation of Isabell. "I'm sure both of you wanted that kept quiet."

"If you're suggesting the either of us killed Isabell to avoid the gossip, it was a little late for that, don't you think?"

Eleanor looked confused for a minute. One of the other ladies nudged her to keep her talking. "Oh, well, yes, but she was going to see to it that you were both fired from your positions. That seems to be a pretty good motive for wanting her dead."

Cady nodded. "If there is a reason to fire either of us, killing Isabell wouldn't keep that from happening. Isabell made sure everyone heard what she had to say. You need to talk to the town council and the school board with your complaints instead of coming in here harassing me. Killing her put us at the top of the suspect list. That wouldn't be a very wise move on our parts." The conversation wasn't making a lot of sense. "Is there something else you would like to discuss?"

"What about your father and half-brother? I'm sure they weren't happy with what Isabell was saying."

"I'm sure they weren't." Cady agreed. "I haven't spoken to either of them this morning. Most folks in this town have been the target of gossip over the years. I don't think anyone liked it. If being a gossip makes someone a target, certain people should be watching their back right about now." The four women shuffled their feet, keeping their eyes trained on the floor. "If there's nothing else, I need to get back to work. Have a nice day, ladies." She stood up, indicating the conversation is over.

They took several steps away from Cady's desk but didn't leave the library. They huddled together, discussing their next move. "Well, that didn't go as expected," Tilly huffed, giving Eleanor's arm a slap. "You should have been more forceful. Isabell never would have let Cady talk to her like that."

"And look where it got her," Eleanor sighed. "We need to regroup." She turned on her heel and marched out of the library. The other ladies followed her like a bunch of lemmings following the leader. They hadn't gotten what they came here for, but how long before they came back? Maybe one of the other women would try to pressure her into answering their questions.

Looking at those sitting close to her desk, she held her head up. She hadn't killed Isabell and she wasn't going to be intimidated by their questioning stares. It appeared that Eleanor was quickly becoming the gossip maven of Tumbleweed. If Isabell had been killed because she was spreading gossip, Eleanor might want to watch her back.

But who would kill someone over gossip? The things Isabell had said about them were true. Olivia did have an affair with Mason Jarvis while he was married, and she had a baby. How did Isabell or Eleanor hope to benefit from that? Was it simply the thrill of knowing things about people that drove someone like Isabell?

She sighed. What would they do if she and Olivia were fired? She didn't know about the school, but she didn't think there was a morality clause in her contract with the town.

She shook her head. Even if there was such a thing, she couldn't be held responsible for what her parents had done twenty-two years ago. Could she? Had she slipped through a time warp where children were blamed for what their parents did?

When someone cleared his throat, Cady gave a startled jump. "Oh, Pastor Bryan I'm sorry. I didn't see you standing there. How are you? Do you need help with something?"

He shook his head. "I came to see if there was anything I can do for you." He paused to look at the people straining to eavesdrop on their conversation. Several people had the decency to move away from Cady's desk.

Standing up, Cady led him to the small workroom. He followed her but not before casting a disapproving look at those still trying to listen in on their conversation. "As I'm sure you're aware, the busybodies are out in force," he said once they were away from the prying eyes and ears. "Isabell felt it was her job to spread every juicy tidbit she heard." He shook his head again. "I tried to tell her that someday gossiping would come back and bite her. She simply wouldn't listen. She's answering to God now for all the times she has hurt people by spreading gossip and lies."

"Thank you." Hot tears burned at the back of her eyes. No one enjoyed having the darkest secrets of their lives brought into the light of day. "The truth would have eventually come out after Mr. Jarvis came here. The part that hurts the most is that Mom didn't feel she could tell me this a long time ago." A single tear slipped down her cheek and she brushed it away.

Pastor Bryan patted her hand. "Yes, it would have come out, but Isabell enjoyed spreading it around far more than anyone should have. I can't speculate as to why your mom never told you about your father. I'm sure she thought it was the best way to protect you at the time. We all make mistakes in our lives, some more than others. Olivia is a good woman. Remember that she loves you very much. If there is anything I can do for you, my door is always open."

"You might want to warn Eleanor," Cady said. "She and the other ladies from the book club have already paid me a visit this morning. I'm not sure what she has in mind, but she was repeating some of the things Isabell said yesterday. They seem to think Mom and I should both lose our jobs."

Looking down at the floor as though saying a silent prayer, he shook his head. "I'll talk with her and the other ladies. I can't guarantee it will do any more good than it did with Isabell, but I will try." Giving her hand another comforting pat, he left her alone.

Why couldn't more people be like Pastor Bryan? He didn't judge her or her mom. He just wanted to help in any way he could.

It was later in the day when a detective from the sheriff's department came to see her. His lightweight jacket covered the gun at his hip. He had the same bearing that Darrell had. Looking at either of them, you immediately knew they were law enforcement. In his mid-to-late thirties, the laugh lines around his eyes and mouth meant he laughed a lot.

"Hello, Miss Townsend. I'm Detective Rodriguez with the Sheriff's Office." He paused to look around. "I see you have a pretty full house today. Is there someplace we can talk privately? Human nature what it is, I'm sure these good people would be eavesdropping on our conversation." His voice was loud enough that those closest to her desk were able to hear. Cady felt a touch of satisfaction when she saw several of them blush at his intentional jab.

Standing up, she led him to the workroom. It had been doubling as her office in recent weeks. Once the door was closed, she offered him a seat and sat down opposite him. "What can I do for you, Detective?"

"I just need to verify some information." She nodded for him to continue. "I've already spoken with Mr. Jarvis and his son. He confirmed the stories circulating about him and your mom." Unsure what she was supposed to say, Cady simply nodded. "Where were you between the hours of midnight and five-thirty this morning?"

"I spent the night at my friend's apartment. Her name is Blair Ratcliff."

"She's a nurse at the community hospital?" he asked. She wasn't surprised that he knew her. In a town the size of Tumbleweed, it's hard not to know most everyone in town.

"Yes. We talked until around midnight and then we went to sleep. We both had to get up for work this morning."

"Why did you spend the night at your friend's apartment instead of at home?"

She was willing to bet he already knew she had been upset that Mason and Jerrod were with her mom when she got home. He still wanted to hear her side of it. According to all the cop shows on TV, you should always have a lawyer with you when the police question you even if you haven't done anything wrong. That would just prolong the inevitable and make it look like she had something to hide.

"As you know, Isabell had made sure everyone in town knew that I am the illegitimate daughter of Mr. Jarvis." For once she didn't cringe at that term. Maybe she was getting used to thinking that. "She said we should be fired from our jobs. When I got home, Mason and Jerrod Jarvis were with my mom while she fixed dinner. I over-reacted and stormed out. I went to stay with Blair." She sighed. "I didn't know what happened to Isabell until this morning." She wouldn't tell him that Darrell had called with the news. She didn't want to get him in trouble.

"Why did Mrs. Brewster think she could get you fired? If being illegitimate was against the law, there would be a lot of us in jail."

Was he including himself? she wondered. She shrugged. "I don't know, but if you know anything about Isabell, this wasn't the first time she'd tried to ruin someone with her gossip." She wasn't sure how far Isabell's reputation and reach went. But Detective Rodriguez knew Blair, so maybe he also knew a lot about Isabell.

"Do you think there are a lot of people who want her

dead?" he asked.

"I wouldn't say they wanted her dead, but over the years a lot of people have been hurt by the tales she's spread around."

"Were any of her rumors and gossip sufficient to want her dead?" he pressed.

She shook her head. "I have no idea. Even as a teenager I knew enough not to listen to what she said. When she wasn't trying to dig up dirt on people, she was reasonably nice." That wasn't very often, but Cady kept that to herself.

Guessing at her thoughts, a deep chuckle rumbled in the detective's broad chest. "A few weeks ago, someone shot at you, and a couple of days later the vehicle you were riding in was run off the road by a hit and run driver. The suspect or suspects in both cases still haven't been found." It wasn't a question so she didn't say anything.

"At the time, you told Deputy Flanagan that Robert Gaston was upset with you. You also mentioned Jerrod Jarvis as a possible suspect. Can you think of anyone else who would want to hurt you?"

She'd gone over this with Darrell and the State Trooper at the scene of the accident. Why was he asking again? Didn't he read the reports? "I didn't say Jerrod Jarvis could be a suspect. He wasn't in town at the time. As you can imagine, Jerrod and his sister weren't any happier with me than I was learning about them. That doesn't mean either of them wanted to kill me. I was casually seeing Robert Gaston at the time. What does any of that have to do with Isabell's murder?"

Ignoring her question, he asked one of his own. "Do you know where Mr. Gaston is now? Apparently, there was some question about his name as well."

Cady sighed. "When I met Robert, he said his name was Gates. Of course, he claims I misunderstood him."

"Did you know that he's related to Mr. Jarvis' late wife?"

Cady shook her head. "At the time I met Robert I knew

nothing about Mr. Jarvis. What does this have to do with Isabell's murder?" she asked again.

"Maybe nothing, but I don't like odd coincidences. I'm just trying to make sense of three separate crimes that remain unsolved." He stood up. "If you think of anything else, give me a call." He took a business card out of his pocket and handed it to her.

Alone again, she slumped back in the chair. Did he know she was seeing Darrell? Did it matter? If she was a suspect, he probably wouldn't be able to talk to her until this was cleared up. How had her nice, uncomplicated life suddenly become so complicated?

Remembering what he'd said that morning, a smile lifted her lips and her heart. She was sure her feelings were leaning in the same direction, but with everything else going on she wasn't sure if they would even get the chance to explore the possibility.

When she pulled into the drive at the end of the day, Mason's rental car was right behind her. Sighing, she rested her chin on her chest. As sure as she was about her growing feelings for Darrell, she was equally unsure about her feelings toward Mason and Jerrod.

It had been a long and trying day. She didn't want to get into another fight with her mom or with Mason and his son. But she wasn't going to run away again. She would face them and see what they had to say. Isabell's body had been found in the dumpster behind his hotel. It would be rather stupid of either of them to dump her body there if they'd killed her. Mason said his kids weren't very nice. Maybe they weren't very smart either. And everyone knows you can't fix stupid.

Picking up her purse and book bag, she whispered, "Here goes nothing."

CHAPTER SIXTEEN

Before she could get out of her car, Mason opened the door for her. "Hello, Cady." He spoke softly as though he was afraid he might frighten her.

"Hello." She wasn't sure what else to say. Jerrod stood behind his dad eyeing her with either curiosity or suspicion. Or maybe both. She couldn't decide. He didn't look quite as demented as he had the day he came to the library.

Besides being slightly taller than his father, there was little resemblance between them. Jerrod's hair was almost white blonde where Mason's was as dark as hers. His eyes were a crystal blue instead of the cocoa brown of his father. Hers were somewhere in between the two. Like Jerrod, Cady had gotten her height from Mason since her mom was only five feet five. She wasn't ready to claim him as her father, but she couldn't deny the part heredity had played in her make up.

Realizing she was staring at them, a bright blush crept up her neck. Looking at her feet, she finally spoke up. "Shall we go inside? Mom's watching to make sure we aren't going to get in a brawl here on the driveway." She scraped past them, making sure she didn't make contact. She couldn't help feeling awkward with them.

Mason said Jerrod and his sister had known about her since they were kids. He'd had time to adjust to the fact that he had a half-sister out there somewhere. This was all new to her. She wasn't sure how she felt about it either.

Olivia was standing in the doorway when Cady opened the door. Without saying a word, she pulled her daughter in for a fierce hug. After a minute, she whispered against Cady's ear, "I'm so sorry about last night, about everything. If I could, I'd do so many things differently." Pulling away from Cady without releasing her, she looked her in the eyes. "The one thing I wouldn't do differently was falling in love and having you. You are by far the best thing I've ever done. I hope you believe that."

"I know, Mom. I wish I had questioned you about my father, but it never mattered. There were so many people in my life that loved me, I didn't need a father." Realizing how that sounded, she looked over her shoulder at Mason and Jerrod. "Sorry." A soft blush crept over her cheeks.

Mason chuckled. "As long as we're apologizing, I'd like to add mine to the mix. I've made a lot of mistakes in my life. You aren't one of them."

Jerrod glared at all of them. "Yes," he growled fiercely. "Melanie and I are two of your biggest mistakes."

Mason turned to his son. "No, you and your sister weren't mistakes. The mistake was in letting your mother bully me and everyone around her to get her own way. I should have paid closer attention to what she was doing to both of you. I feel like I've betrayed all three of my children. If I could do things over again, I would have left her and taken the two of you with me before she did any damage. All I can say is I will try to do better from now on. I hope it isn't too late for you and Melanie to give me a chance."

They were still congregated in the doorway and Jerrod squeezed past. It took him several minutes before he said anything. Keeping his back to his father, he spoke softly. "I can't speak for Melanie, but I'm willing to try. You weren't the only one to betray us. The things I've learned since Mother died..." Giving his head a shake, a lock of blonde hair fell over his forehead. "The only person she loved was herself, and maybe her father. I wouldn't swear to that though. Melanie and I were so far down her list of priorities we were barely a blip on her radar." Cady thought he looked like a little boy ready to cry at the admission.

"Where is your daughter?" Cady asked. "Why hasn't she

148

come here to look me over?" She turned to glare at Jerrod.

The two men exchanged a look Cady couldn't interpret. They were silent so long she thought they weren't going to say anything. Mason finally sighed. "Melanie is in rehab for the third or fourth time. Hopefully, it will take this time."

"Rehab only works if the person is ready to admit they need help. It isn't something that can be forced on them," Olivia said.

So many things had happened since he arrived on her birthday she couldn't remember whether he'd already told her Melanie was in rehab.

Mason nodded. "That's why I have hope this time. She signed herself in just days after Belinda's funeral. She doesn't seem to be in a hurry to get out this time either. At least as long as I'm footing the bill," he added with a sigh. "She has refused to see me and won't take my calls." There was a question in his eyes when he looked at his son.

"She doesn't want to see me either. She blames all of us for her drinking problem."

"Then she's not accepting responsibility for her actions," Cady said. "Until she does…" She shrugged, letting the others draw their own conclusions.

It was a strange evening. Mason wanted to know all about Cady's childhood. He'd told her he had been to several of her soccer games while she was in middle school and had attended her high school and college graduations. She didn't know how he had managed that since they were by invitation only. But there was more to her life than soccer and graduations. He wanted to know everything.

Jerrod wanted to know what life was like in a small town. Cade shrugged. "I imagine it isn't much different from life in a big city." She gave a small laugh. "Except everyone knows your business and you know theirs. That doesn't usually turn deadly though," she added the sobering thought.

"Thanks to that woman, I guess the whole town knows about all the skeletons in our family's closet by now." He didn't look pleased about that fact.

An awkward silence descended on them. There was just so much small talk you could make with people you didn't know and had little in common with. Cady knew Mason wanted her to call him dad, but that wasn't going to happen anytime soon. At twenty-one, she didn't need or want someone to step into the role that had never needed filling. She'd be happy if she was eventually able to accept him as a friend and part of her life.

It wasn't hard to see that Olivia was still in love with him. Looking back over her life, she realized he was the reason she had seldom dated. What about Mason? Was he still in love with Olivia? She didn't want her mom to get her heart broken a second time by the same man.

What would it mean if he was still in love with her? Would they get married? Would Olivia leave Tumbleweed? She didn't want to think about that.

They'd been avoiding the elephant in the room all evening. Maybe it was time to talk about Isabell's murder. The detective told each of them not to talk to others about what happened, but since they were all probably at the top of his suspect list, she didn't see how it could hurt.

"Do you have security cameras posted around the outside of the hotel?" She looked at Mason. When he nodded, she continued. "Did they pick up anything useful?" The detective hadn't given her any indication one way or the other.

"No, unfortunately, the killer managed to avoid all of the cameras. The one pointed toward the dumpsters had been disabled." He sighed. "The desk clerk was going to check it out this morning. Of course by then, it was too late."

"Whoever did this must have known where the cameras were," Olivia said. "Does anyone but your employees have that kind of information?"

"All of the employees should be aware of the camera locations, but I can't see one of them doing this. The hotel hasn't been open long enough to have disgruntled employees. I've gone through all of the personnel records and the detective spent a good part of the day interviewing everyone that works at the hotel. The only employee that has been fired is Robert. I'd say he has plenty of grievances against me, but murder seems a little extreme even for him."

"Do you know if he's is still in town?"

"I have no idea. I gave the detective his name and any information I had in his personnel file." He looked at Cady and Jerrod. "Has he tried to contact either of you?"

Cady shook her head. "The last time I saw him was the day after my birthday. It didn't go well. By now he must realize I know about his lies. He's smart enough to know I don't want anything to do with him."

"I have a few choice words I'd like to say to him after what he and Mother tried to pull," Jerrod said. "But I haven't heard anything from him. If he's still in town, he has to know I'm here."

"Do either of you think he's capable of murdering Isabell?" Olivia asked softly.

Cady shook her head. "Since I didn't realize every word out of his mouth was a lie, I'm not in a position to know whether he's capable of killing someone." Obviously, she wasn't a good judge of character, or she would have known he was lying to her.

What did that say about her feelings for Darrell? He said he was falling in love with her. How was she supposed to know when someone was telling her the truth? She'd never had reason to wonder if someone was lying to her until now. Other than as a friend, she hadn't had any feelings for Robert, she reminded herself. Did that make a difference?

151

She pushed aside her doubts for now. As long as she and her family were suspects in Isabell's murder, she probably wouldn't be seeing much of Darrell.

"Why would Robert kill her?" Cady asked, "What would it accomplish?"

"It points the finger of guilt at me," Mason answered, looking at each of them. "She was gossiping about us, all of us. Her body was dumped behind the hotel I own and where I'm staying."

"But only a stupid person would dump the body of someone they'd killed where it would make them look guilty," Cady argued. "You don't strike me as being stupid. I don't understand the motive behind killing her. If one of us was going to kill her, why wait until after she made sure everyone heard about us. It isn't like she had to embellish the story to make us look bad either. What she said about us was the truth. So why kill her?"

Her head was beginning to ache. Trying to figure out who killed Isabell and why was making her head hurt and she rubbed her temple.

"Even twenty-one years ago, having an affair with a married man wasn't worth killing someone to keep it secret," Olivia said. She looked at Mason. "If you had been the president of the United States, maybe, but that wasn't the case. I'm not saying what I did was right but once the cat was out of the bag, I don't see what killing Isabell accomplished."

"Does her murder have anything to do with the two attempts on Cady's life?" Jerrod asked the question.

The detective had questioned whether there was a connection between the attempts on her life and Isabell's murder. But she couldn't see how they could be connected.

"I'd never met the woman except for that day in the library. Whoever killed her was probably trying to make me look guilty. After all, with another sibling in the mix, it would eventually cut down on my inheritance."

"Hold on." Cady held up her hand to stop that line of thinking. "I have no right to anything of your father's. I would never do something like that."

"Whether you want to admit it or not, I am your father," Mason said. The hurt her words caused was undeniable. "That means you have a share in anything that I would eventually leave behind."

"No." She shook her head hard enough to dislodge the clip holding her hair in place causing her dark hair to fall into her eyes. She brushed it away impatiently. "That isn't right. I just met you."

"Yes, but I've known about you all of your life. You have been listed as one of my heirs since the day you were born."

"No. Just because you knew about me doesn't mean I should be entitled to anything."

Mason started to argue when a sharp whistle drew their attention. "As nice as all this sounds," Jerrod said. "We still need to think about who would want to kill Cady." Olivia took her daughter's hand. Her fingers were ice cold.

Cady rubbed at her stomach where a swarm of bees had suddenly taken up residence. Yes, someone had shot at her and run her and her friends off the road, supposedly in an attempt to harm her. But she hadn't really believed someone wanted her dead. "How is that related to Isabell's murder?" she whispered. "No one knew about my connection to either of you when I was shot at and run off the road."

"I knew about you," Jerrod stated simply. "I wasn't in Tumbleweed when either attempt was made on your life. I'm sure the police have looked into my finances to see if I made any large withdrawals recently." He turned to look at his father. "I didn't have anything to do with that. I swear."

Mason nodded. "I believe you. But we're forgetting someone else who knows Cady is my daughter. Belinda knew and by extension, Robert knew." He sighed. "Everything that is happening can be traced back to your mother. It's like she's reaching out from the grave in an attempt to ruin everything and everyone I hold dear. She never cared who got hurt as long as she got what she wanted."

"Why would Belinda want to implicate Jerrod in a murder scheme?" Olivia asked. "He's her son."

"Because she didn't care about me," Jerrod stated. "She only cared about herself." With a weary sigh, he rested his head on the back of the chair. "I never realized just how much she hated all of us until recently." He was talking to the ceiling. "She manipulated everyone."

"There is someone else we're all forgetting." Without looking at Mason or Jerrod, Cady asked, "Are you sure Melanie is still in rehab? You said she won't talk to either of you. Is it possible that she's behind all of this? You said Belinda manipulated everyone. If she convinced Robert to do her bidding, maybe she convinced Melanie as well."

Mason's face lost all color. That could be the reason he was never able to talk to her when he called the facility. She had checked herself in; she could also check herself out. If she told them not to let him know she'd left, they wouldn't be able to tell him anything because of privacy restrictions.

Standing up, he took his phone out of his pocket as he began pacing around the room. "This is Mason Jarvis. I need to speak to the administrator about my daughter." He paused, listening to someone on the other end of the line "I don't care what time it is. Let me talk to someone in charge."

It took several minutes, but he was finally connected to someone higher up the food chain than the night receptionist. Explaining what he needed to know and why didn't get him what he wanted. "I realize you can't tell me about her medical or mental condition, but I'm still paying the bill." His voice rang with authority. "Either you tell me whether she is still there and if she has left the facility at any time during her stay, or I will no longer be sending you a check each month."

That got the results he wanted, and he heard the soft clicking as the person checked the computer. Whatever the person said relieved his fears. "Thank you for checking. Please keep the reason for my call as confidential as you keep Melanie's records. Has she had any visitors since she checked in?" Giving a relieved sigh, he thanked the person on the other end of the phone. "Please tell her I called and that I love her."

He turned to look at the others. "She's still in rehab and hasn't left the facility since she checked in a month ago. Jerrod and I are the only people who have attempted to see her." He sank down on the couch beside Olivia taking her hand.

This wasn't getting them any closer to figuring out who or why Isabell had been killed and whether her murder was tied to the attempts on Cady's life.

It was late by the time Mason and Jerrod finally left. Cady's head was throbbing. Taking two ibuprofen, she made her way upstairs. As tired as she was, she couldn't shut her mind off. She'd been letting her personal drama overshadow Isabell's murder. Why had she been killed? If it was because of what she was saying about Cady and Olivia, why kill her after she revealed their secret? Killing Isabell wouldn't stop the talk. Eleanor's visit that morning was proof of that. She was stepping into Isabell's shoes before the woman was even cold.

The only person she could think of who would want to frame Mason or Jerrod was Robert. But how would that benefit him? Even if either one or both of them went to prison, Robert would have no claim on Jarvis House Hotels. Where was he? No one had seen him since Mason fired him. Would he kill someone in cold blood? A shiver moved down her spine.

It was past two in the morning when she fell into a fitful sleep. When she woke the next morning she was as tired as she'd been when she went to bed.

CHAPTER SEVENTEEN

Olivia was still dressed in her robe when she came into the kitchen. School was out for the summer. She had to go in to clean out her classroom so the maintenance crews could do deep cleaning and make any repairs necessary, but not until a little later. Would she have a job when the summer was over? Did it matter? What were Mason's intentions toward her? Her heart did a little stutter step.

If the smoldering looks he sent in her direction meant anything, his feelings for her hadn't changed much in twenty-two years. She knew he still owned her heart. But they weren't the same people they'd been.

They had each grown and changed. Would those changes make a difference in how they felt about each other? Only time would tell. Their lives had gone in opposite directions. She and Cady had made a life in Tumbleweed. His life was in San Francisco and wherever his hotels were located.

One thing she knew, she wouldn't jump into a relationship the way she had before. She would take her time to make sure of what the future could hold for them.

"Good morning, Honey." She placed a kiss on top of Cady's head. She had started the coffee and was on her second cup. After a restless night, she needed something to help wake her up. "You look like you didn't get much sleep last night," she stated the obvious.

Cady nodded. "There were too many things on my mind."

"I hope you weren't upset that I had invited Mason and Jerrod here for dinner again. You need to get to know them. At least get to know Mason. He is your father."

"Yes, so everyone keeps telling me. You can't expect me to immediately embrace that fact. It's going to take time."

"Oh, Honey, I wish I could undo the way I handled things

when you were little. But I can't."

"I know. It's all right, Mom. Something else is taking priority over that right now. I'm pretty sure most of the people in town are going to be thinking one of us, or all of us killed Isabell." She hadn't heard from Darrell since her body had been found. What did that mean? Did he subscribe to that theory? Had he been told he couldn't see her as long as she was a suspect? Or had that been his decision? It probably wouldn't do his career any good to be seen with a potential murder suspect.

"But what motive would we have to kill Isabell?" Olivia asked. It was the same argument she'd had the night before. "The truth was out. Killing her after the fact doesn't make any sense."

"Neither does someone trying to kill me because of who Mason is. But if it wasn't Jerrod or Melanie, who else would have a reason to want me dead?" Her voice cracked slightly. "I know we talked about Robert last night. But that doesn't make sense either. He didn't have any feelings for me. He was just trying to get close to me because of my... because of Mason," she finished. She refused to call him her dad.

"I'm a librarian in a small town. I don't have anything someone else could want. Unless someone wanted my job bad enough to kill for, that is." The thought was almost laughable. It wasn't exactly a coveted position. She would never get rich being head librarian in their small town. That wasn't why she'd accepted the job.

"What are we going to do if the town council and school board decide to fire us because of... you know?" That worry had been in the back of her mind.

"That isn't going to happen," Olivia stated with certainty.

"But if it does? What are we going to do?" Seeing the answer on her mom's face, she held up her hand. "Don't say that Mason will take care of us. We've never let a man do that.

I'm not about to start now."

"Are you becoming a feminist?" Olivia asked with a chuckle.

"No." She drew the word out. "It just doesn't feel right to take money from him. I just found out he's my birth father. Besides, isn't that what Jerrod was afraid of when he came here: that I was after his father's money. He called me a gold digger." It would be a long while before she was able to forget the look of disgust on his face when he said those words.

"He's your father, too," she said gently. "Anyone who knows you knows you aren't a gold digger." When Cady would have objected, she pushed on.

"Honey, he's been sending us money your entire life. I tried to tell you that after Mason came here. You were too angry to listen. Every summer vacation we took was with money Mason sent. He also sent child support every month. I put it away for your college tuition." She sighed. "He even paid your full tuition each year. I still have all of the money he sent in savings for you."

"Give it back to him. I don't want it." Cady pushed away from the table, sending her chair across the floor.

"Cady Elizabeth Townsend, sit down." When Olivia used her full name she knew she was in for a lecture. "Stop acting like a spoiled brat. You need to hear what I have to say."

"I've heard it, Mom. You fell in love, you got pregnant. I was born. You never mentioned that I had a father who was paying for everything I ever did or had." This felt like another betrayal.

"Yes, he paid for a lot of things for you, for us. He did it because he loved us. He still does."

Cady gasped. "Are you going to marry him?" Her eyes misted over. Her whole life was being turned upside down.

"I don't know what is going to happen between Mason and me," Olivia said with a sigh. "As you can imagine, we haven't had a lot of time to discuss what's next for the two of us. I'm not going to jump into anything," she assured her daughter. "I guess a lot depends on what happens here."

Cady stood up again. "I need to get ready for work. Are you inviting them for dinner again?"

"If I do, will you be here?" There was a stubborn set to her mother's mouth that she hadn't seen in a long time. She was daring Cady to continue acting like a brat. *What would she do then?* Cady wondered.

"I'll be here," Cady stated softly. "I understand you want to spend time with Mason, but why does Jerrod have to be here as well?"

"He's alone in a strange town. You can't expect him to spend all of his time in the hotel suite while his dad comes here for dinner."

Cady huffed for a minute. "Dinner was always when we discussed our day and what we were going to do the next day. Any plans we had we made over dinner. Now they're here. Maybe I'm a little jealous," she grudgingly admitted. "I don't like sharing you with him."

Olivia laughed. "Honey, someday you're going to find a man who will love you and take you away from me. I'll miss all the times we've spent together. But that's the way life is supposed to work. I would never want to hold you back from having a life of your own. I hope you feel the same."

"Of course I do," Cady said with a sigh. She had been hoping Darrell would turn out to be that man. Would this mess prevent any relationship from happening? She placed a kiss on her mom's cheek. "I need to get dressed."

Olivia sighed. Another crisis averted. Her normal, dull life had suddenly become anything but dull.

Martha was waiting for Cady when she got to the library. "I stopped for coffee before coming in this morning." She handed Cady a to-go cup.

160

"Thank you?" There was a question in her voice. Something was up. Martha didn't usually stop to get coffee, and she'd never brought Cady a cup before.

"Okay. What's going on?" She wasn't sure she wanted to know about it, but there was no getting out of it. She took a cautious sip of the hot liquid.

"I'm sure you're not aware of this, but my husband and I were friends with Eleanor and her husband when they first moved to town ten years ago. Her husband had an affair with a much younger woman and she got pregnant. I'm not sure if that was his first affair or the first pregnancy, but he left Eleanor and married this woman.

"For a very long time, Eleanor hated men, all men. I'm not sure she ever stopped hating them." She sighed. "As you can imagine, our friendship didn't last after that. Not because Fred and I didn't want to be friends," she added. "We tried to stay friends with her. But she wanted nothing to do with people she'd known while she was married. That's also when she starting palling around with Isabell."

"I'm sorry about that, but what does that have to do with now?" She wasn't sure where Martha was going with this. When all of that was going on in Eleanor's life, Cady had been eleven. Gossip hadn't meant anything to her.

"I hope you don't think I'm turning into a gossip like Isabell. That's not why I'm telling you this. I just think you should have a little background. You need to know what's going on." Martha sighed heavily. "Eleanor has taken over where Isabell left off. In fact, she's taking this a step further. It's almost like Isabell has invaded her body and she's now Isabell on steroids."

Cady sank down onto her desk chair. The library wouldn't open for another hour. They had work that needed to be done, but this might be more important. "Okay. What is Eleanor saying about me?"

"Not just you," Martha said. "She said she's done a little surfing on the internet which can be dangerous," she added. "She said that Mr. Jarvis's wife died recently."

Cady nodded. There was nothing scandalous about that. When Martha paused, her breakfast threatened to put in a return appearance. "What else is Eleanor saying?"

Martha sighed. "She said the woman died under suspicious circumstances and it was covered up because he's wealthy. According to Eleanor, the wealthy always get a pass."

"That's a lie," Cady sputtered. "Why would she say something like that?"

"The fact that your mom had an affair with Mr. Jarvis while he was married brought back some very bad memories for her. She wants all men to pay for what her husband did. Especially those who cheat. That's another reason I stopped trying to be friends with her. She had turned into a very bitter woman. Usually she doesn't have much to say, but when something comes on the news about a famous man cheating on his wife, she turns into a totally different person. I'm sorry."

Cady felt like her head was going to explode. "She seemed so meek the day Isabell sent her in to grill me about Jerrod." Of course, that was before anyone knew she was Mason Jarvis' illegitimate daughter. She still didn't know who had let that cat out of the bag.

Martha nodded her head. "That's the way she usually is, even ten years ago. I don't know what happened between Eleanor and her husband that caused him to cheat. They hadn't lived here long before he left her. She usually calms down after a few days and the media drops the coverage, but I'm afraid that isn't going to happen now. You and your mom live here. Eleanor sees you all the time. I'm not sure where she's going to go with this, but you might want to warn your mom and dad."

"He isn't my dad," Cady automatically objected. "Well, he is," she said with a sigh. "I can't think of him like that, not yet anyway. I still don't want him railroaded because Eleanor's husband left her for another woman. I'll call Mom. Thanks for letting me know." She held up the cup of coffee. "Thanks for this, too. I think I'm going to need several more before the day is over."

After learning about Mason, Cady had done her own research. There was nothing online about his wife's cause of death, suspicious or otherwise. Where had Eleanor gotten that idea? Was this her way of smearing a man that had cheated on his wife? Mason wasn't into politics. She'd been unable to find anything that indicated he had a lot of political friends. How could he have covered up the fact that he had something to do with his wife's death without a lot of help from higher up?

What would Mason or Jerrod do if Eleanor started spreading a lot of vicious rumors about them? If Isabell had been killed because of what she'd said about her mom and Mason, what would that person do to Eleanor? Cady's head was spinning and the library hadn't even opened yet.

Going into the workroom, she called her mom. If Eleanor was telling people that Mason had possibly killed his wife so he could be with Olivia, she needed to know. Olivia wasn't surprised by this information. She remembered some sort of scandal involving Eleanor's husband. She didn't know or didn't remember the details, but she did remember Isabell had all but run the man and his new wife out of town with the things she was saying. She hadn't been kind to Eleanor either.

If Isabell had done that, why would Eleanor become friends with her? What would Eleanor gain by expanding on Isabell's gossip? Was she hoping to run Mason and Jerrod out of town? What would that accomplish? What about Cady and Olivia? Was she also hoping they would leave Tumbleweed?

What good would any of that do Eleanor? Her head was aching and the day had barely started.

Finally able to lock the door at five o'clock, Cady sighed with relief. Three days a week the library was open until seven. She was grateful this wasn't one of those days. It had still been busy with people coming and going hoping to learn something about Isabell's murder. Cady didn't know how anyone expected her to know anything though. Even if the police didn't consider her a suspect, they wouldn't tell her anything. Thankfully, Eleanor didn't put in an appearance.

Cady's thoughts were still jumbled up as she made her way to her car behind the library. The dumpster Henry had called home for several months was still unoccupied. She supposed that was a good thing. Not all of the homeless population was as neat and tidy about their surroundings and person as Henry was. What was he doing now? She wished him well. Isabell had been extremely cruel when dealing with people she felt were beneath her. *People like Henry*, Cady thought. He hadn't been hurting anything by staying there.

She'd seen the trash left behind at some of the homeless encampments. They grumbled when they were chased off. If they picked up after themselves, that might not happen so often. Henry had always been considerate of others. She'd even seen him run other homeless off when they tried to encroach on his site. She shook her head. Maybe he didn't like living in squalor either. She said a small prayer that he'd found somewhere safe to stay.

Thoughts about Henry were driven from her mind when she saw Darrell's big truck parked beside her car. He was leaning casually against the door, one ankle crossed over the other. A sexy grin quirked his lips up as she walked toward him. Her heart was in her throat making it difficult to breathe. The smile said he wasn't here to arrest her.

"Hi?" Her doubts turned the single word into a question.

164

How far had Eleanor's lies spread in a single day?

"Hi, yourself. How are you holding up?" Without standing up, he took her hand, pulling her close enough to place a soft kiss on his lips.

"As well as can be expected," she answered. She heard the breathlessness in her voice. The simple kiss had rocked her to the soles of her feet. "Have you been able to figure out who killed Isabell?"

He shook his head. "I'm not part of the investigation."

"Because of me," she guessed.

"Yeah, partly," he admitted. "But don't let it worry you. Detective Rodriguez isn't one to share his investigation with a lowly deputy." He chuckled. "Now tell me about your day. How are you really doing?" He pulled her closer so she was leaning against him.

Martha's warning came to mind instantly. "I suppose you've heard the latest gossip." He nodded and she went on. "I'm not sure if you know who Eleanor Davis is, but she's taken Isabell's place as gossip-in-charge. I have it on good authority that she can be as vicious as Isabell when it comes to gossip."

"What's her deal? Why's she spreading a bunch of lies?"

"Apparently, she doesn't like men who cheat on their wives or the women they cheat with. That means she doesn't like my mom or Mason Jarvis."

"What does she have to say about the offspring of said cheaters?" A dark frown furrowed his brow. "Words can be just as damaging as slings and arrows. Telling a bunch of libelous lies can also get her into trouble with the law. She could find herself being sued if she isn't careful." They stood like that for several minutes, each contemplating the consequences of those lies.

He wasn't there to discuss the latest gossip. "Do you have plans for dinner?"

A smile lit up her face. "Not anything that can't be changed. I'll need to call my mom." Remembering her conversation with Olivia that morning, she sighed. "Mason and Jerrod have been having dinner with Mom for the past few nights. I haven't been a very gracious hostess. I walked out the first night, but I did stay around last night."

"How did that turn out?"

She shrugged. "Okay, I guess. I managed not to kill anyone if that counts for anything." He chuckled when she sighed. "I don't know how long it's going to take for me to accept everything I've learned in the last couple of weeks."

She pulled out of his arms. "I'll call and tell her I have a better offer for dinner. I'm sure she'll understand." She crossed her fingers, hoping that wasn't a lie. "I'm twenty-one. You'd think I wouldn't have to get approval from my mom to go on a date." Her face grew warm. "That is what this is, right?"

"Most definitely." He ran a finger down the side of her face.

Stepping further away from him, she took her phone out of her pocket. She had told her mom she would be there for dinner. She hoped Olivia wouldn't think she was chickening out. Considering their conversation that morning, she shouldn't be unhappy. After all, she said Cady would eventually be leaving the nest.

"Hi, Mom. I hope you don't mind if I beg off dinner. It has nothing to do with Mason and Jerrod being there," she quickly added. "I've… got a date." She listened for a minute before going on. "No, I don't think that's a good idea. He's um, a sheriff's deputy." Again she paused. "Yes, the one that brought me home the night someone shot at me. We've sort of been seeing each other." She was surprised her mom hadn't heard that piece of gossip since Isabell had seen them together. Ending the call, she turned back to Darrell.

166

"Everything clear at home?" He raised one eyebrow.

"She suggested we have dinner with them. I saved you from an inquisition." She shook her head. "Living in a town small enough that she knew the parents of all the boys I dated saved them from the game of twenty questions. But you're new here. I'm sure she would have plenty of questions for you. I'm not sure what Mason would have to say either." She shuddered slightly at the thought of him becoming an over-protective father.

Darrell chuckled. "I remember a few of those conversations. I guess that sort of thing goes along with being the parent of a daughter. Where would you like to eat?" He changed the subject.

CHAPTER EIGHTEEN

The summer tourist season was in full swing. That meant there was a waiting list at most of the restaurants. Even the places few tourists knew about were crowded. "I hope you aren't hungry," she said when she saw the number of customers sitting on the benches in front of Manuel's Mexican Restaurant.

"As long as they don't run out of food, I don't mind," he joked. "I said the back patio was fine. I hope that's all right?"

"Perfect." She smiled up at him. They were less likely to draw attention sitting on the patio than inside. She didn't want to run into Eleanor.

By mutual consent, they avoided talk of Isabell's murder. Neither of them wanted to ruin a perfectly good dinner. Instead of lingering at the table when they finished eating, they quickly left. There was still a line waiting to be seated. Not wanting to call it a night, they strolled down the sidewalk hand-in-hand. Cady couldn't ask for a better night. There were plenty of people around, but no one paid attention to them. If Eleanor was out and about, they were lucky enough not to run into her.

"I have a pretty crazy schedule," Darrell said as they headed back to his truck. "What days are you off?"

"The library is closed on Sunday and is open only a half-day on Saturday. I also take a half-day off during the week. I don't usually have a set day for that. What are you suggesting?" She mentally crossed her fingers, hoping he was asking her out again.

"I thought you might like to show me some of your favorite hiking trails. You did say you enjoyed hiking, right? Just not in high heels and a dress," he teased.

Her face turned a pretty shade of pink. "Yes, I do. I even

168

know of some trails the tourists haven't found yet."

"Sounds better all the time." A smile lifted his lips. Her heart began to race at the memory of those lips pressed against hers. "I'm off on Wednesday and Thursday next week. Could you manage a full day off?"

"I think I can do that. Martha is always willing to take over if I need extra time off. We have several volunteers who enjoy coming in to help out as well."

Pulling into the parking lot behind the library, Cady gasped as the headlights on the big truck moved over her much smaller car. Tiny sparks flashed from the broken glass littering the ground. Vulgar words had been spray-painted on the sides and trunk of the car. "Who would do that?" Angry tears burned the back of her eyes.

"Stay in the truck," Darrell ordered. "I need to make sure no one is waiting for you to come back." He was out before she could argue. Within minutes he was back confirming the damage to her car. "All four tires are slashed and every window has been smashed. There is spray paint on the sides, hood, and trunk." He sighed. "I'm sorry about this. We shouldn't have left it here."

"This isn't your fault." While he'd been inspecting her car, she had tried to think of who would do something like this. There were only two people she could think of: Eleanor Davis and Robert Gaston.

Mason had fired Robert and was fighting his claim that the hotel belonged to him. But that didn't explain why he would do this to her car. She was Mason Jarvis's illegitimate daughter. Did that make her a target in Eleanor's eyes? This didn't make sense.

There were no security cameras in the back parking lot. Until now there hadn't been a need for them. If Isabell had left Henry alone, this wouldn't have happened. He would have run the vandals off before they could do any damage.

A deputy's SUV pulled up behind Darrell's truck and they both got out. After taking all the necessary information, the deputy called for a tow truck. Nothing else could be done until morning. She'd have to call her insurance company and get a rental. At least the car was still mechanically sound. She crossed her fingers. *I hope.*

"I'll take you home," Darrell said as he helped her get in the high truck. "You need to warn your mom and Mr. Jarvis that something like this might happen to their vehicles as well." He stopped short of calling Mason her dad knowing it would upset her further. "I can't believe an elderly woman would do something like this." She'd given the other deputy Eleanor and Robert's names. It still didn't feel right. Why would either of them do this? "It seems more like a bunch of juvenile delinquents out for some fun."

If only, she thought. She shook her head, disagreeing with him. "We've never had a problem here with juvenile delinquency before," she said. Until recently, the crime rate in Tumbleweed was relatively low.

"Eleanor isn't exactly elderly either, maybe her late fifties." Cady shook her head. "If you're asking for my opinion, I think either Eleanor or Robert had a hand in this." Eleanor was becoming more demented by the day. "But what does this accomplish?" Nothing was making any sense.

The rumble of the diesel engine as they pulled into the driveway at home drew the attention Cady had been hoping to avoid. The thought of telling her mom and Mason about what happened caused her stomach to hurt. Her mom would be upset, but she had no idea how Mason or Jerrod would react. Jerrod had changed since that day in the library. Was it an act, or would he be upset for her? She had her fingers crossed that Mason wouldn't act like an over-protective father.

"Cady?" Olivia was standing in the kitchen when they came in the back door. "Did something happen to your car?

Were you in an accident?" Worry clouded her eyes.

"I'm fine, Mom. Do you remember Deputy Darrell Flanagan? Darrell, this is my mom, Olivia Townsend." She groaned softly when Mason stepped up behind Olivia. This gave her flashbacks of the night Darrell had brought her home when someone shot at her in the forest.

"I'm Mason Jarvis, but you already know that." He stretched out his hand to Darrell. "What's going on?"

At least he hadn't said he was her dad, Cady thought. "Someone vandalized my car while we were having dinner. Darrell brought me home." She was hoping they would leave it at that. She should have known better.

"The same person who killed Isabell?" Mason asked. One eyebrow arched up. By now, Jerrod had joined them in the kitchen. He gave Darrell a curt nod but didn't say anything. He was still upset that Darrell had hauled him out of the library and taken him to the station for questioning. He should be grateful that he hadn't been arrested.

"We don't know who did it, Sir. We left her car in the library parking lot while we were at dinner. I called the department to make a report. A forensic team will go over it in the morning hoping to collect some useable prints. It's a long shot." He shrugged.

"Are you getting any closer to finding out who killed Isabell?" Olivia asked.

"I'm not working the case," Darrell said. "But I don't believe the suspect left much evidence behind. She was killed somewhere else and placed in the dumpster. That's all I know."

"That's all you know or all you can say?" Mason frowned at him.

"Both. But you're right, I can't comment on an active investigation. Sorry." It wasn't an apology, but simply a statement of fact. He wasn't going to let Mason intimidate him.

"Why would anyone do that to your car?" Olivia asked. "Since you didn't drive it home, I'm guessing it isn't drivable."

"I'm going to need four new tires and new windows all around, as well as a paint job." Cady sighed. This wasn't the way she'd hoped the evening would end.

"That sounds like a bunch of teenagers out for some fun," Mason said. In a large city, that would be the answer.

"As I said, the forensic team will go over the car for any evidence. Until we get this figured out, the department will keep an eye on things around the library. I'm not going to let anything happen to Cady. I'll make sure she is safe." Cady took exception to the fact that he was speaking to Mason, not her mom.

"Thanks for bringing me home, Darrell. I'll walk you out." The sudden chill in her voice drew his brows down over his eyes.

"Did I say something wrong?" He waited until they were outside before asking the question. "I almost got frostbite there for a minute."

"If you felt the need to reassure anyone that I would be safe, you should have been talking to my mom, not him."

"Whether you like it or not, he's still your dad. If he's like most of the fathers I know, he will want to make sure you're safe."

She snorted at that but refrained from arguing. Having a father around was going to take some getting used to. *Maybe*, she silently added. She had no idea how long he was going to be sticking around. Eventually, he would have to leave to run his company. *Would he be taking Mom with him?* The thought left her feeling unsettled and sad.

Placing his finger under her chin, he tipped her head up so she was looking at him. "I'm sorry you're upset. He's been aware of you a lot longer than you've been aware of him. Give yourself time. I hope he'll give you time as well. Who knows, you might even like to have a dad who cares and a big brother, too."

"Harrumph." She wasn't sure about that last part. Jerrod wasn't the warm fuzzy type. She thought he'd rather she dropped off the face of the earth than keep her safe.

"Am I forgiven?" He leaned close, placing nibbling kisses on her neck. Goosebumps moved along her arms. Unable to resist, she tilted her head up so her lips met his. Words were no longer necessary. He'd been forgiven.

When the porch light flickered, Cady growled. "What does he think he's doing?" Her mom had never tried that trick even when she'd been in high school.

"Ignore it," Darrell whispered, capturing her lips again.

But the magic was gone. Cady was ready for a fight. If Mason thought he was going to get away with treating her like she was a teenager on her first date, he could think again. "I'll see you tomorrow." She paused, looking at him hopefully. "Maybe?" There was a question in her voice.

"Definitely." He kissed her again. "Don't be too hard on him." Chuckling, he walked to his truck.

Cady pulled the door open, nearly knocking Jerrod over as she stormed inside. "Hey, take it easy." He chuckled.

"Were you the one playing with the lights?" She glared up at him. He wasn't quite as tall as Darrell, but she still had to tip her head back to look him in the eyes.

"Just wanted to see how it feels to be a big brother again," he said with a shrug. A teasing grin played around his full lips. "It got you inside, didn't it?"

"Well, don't get too comfortable. You aren't going to be here that much longer. Besides, you already have a little sister so you don't need to pull that on me."

"Don't think you can get rid of me that fast. I think I'm going to like living in a small town."

"What are you talking about?" Her stomach rolled uncomfortably. A sense of foreboding settled over her.

"I can't live in San Francisco and manage the hotel in Tumbleweed, now can I?"

"Wait. What? Are you moving here?" No, this can't be happening. She turned to glare at Mason. "Ewww." She whirled back around. Her face felt hot. No child, even an adult child, wanted to watch their mom making out. Olivia and Mason were clearly unaware that she and Jerrod might be watching them. Or they simply didn't care.

"What's wrong? Did something happen?" Jerrod stepped around her so he could see into the living room.

"Your father is kissing my mother. That's what's wrong," she whispered harshly.

"No, your mother is kissing *our* father." He chuckled. "I guess they're entitled. They're both single." In all the years his parents had been married, he'd never seen any affection between them. It was a wonder that he and Melanie had been born. One of the many things he'd learned since his mother died was that she had been pregnant at the time they got married. Which one of them had felt trapped in a loveless marriage? Maybe both. He shrugged. After living with Belinda for more than twenty-eight years he figured his old man deserved a little romance.

"I'm going to bed." Cady escaped up the back stairs. Many times she'd been glad there were two staircases in their house. This was one of those times. She was able to escape without disturbing the couple making out in the living room. "Ewww," she whispered again.

~~~

"You disappeared awfully fast last night." Olivia was already in the kitchen when Cady came down the following morning. "Did something happen between you and Jerrod?" She had been hoping that the two siblings would learn to get along.

Instead of answering, Cady asked a question of her own. "Did you know that Jerrod is moving to Tumbleweed? He's taking over as manager at the hotel."

Olivia's face showed genuine surprise before turning to pleasure. "No, Mason never said anything about that. Things have been a little crazy since he came here, so I guess he had other things on his mind."

"Are you going to marry him?" The question tumbled out before Cady could stop it. She couldn't decide how she felt about that possibility. She'd always thought turning twenty-one meant more freedom. Instead, her life had become more complicated. She sighed.

"I'm not sure where our relationship is headed. I promised you before that I wouldn't jump into anything. We still have a lot of things to figure out between us." Her sigh matched Cady's. "One of those things would be where we would live. Mason has his business and he travels a lot. But if you're wondering whether I still love him, the answer is yes. I always have. For some people there is only one love in their life. That's the way it has always been for me. I'd rather remain alone than marry someone I don't love. I'm sorry if that upsets you." She looked at her daughter wishing things had been different twenty-two years ago and now.

Cady shook her head. "I want you to be happy, Mom. I guess if that means you move away from Tumbleweed, I can live with that. It just feels weird right now."

Olivia laughed. "I'll accept weird. It's better than having you upset with me. That's all I can hope for right now. I do hope you will eventually learn to like Mason if you can't love him as your father. As long as he's in Tumbleweed, we're going to be spending a lot of time together." Her voice turned serious. "Until the police find out who tried to hurt you and whether that has anything to do with Isabell's murder, Mason isn't going anywhere. He won't leave either of us unprotected." Cady didn't want to think about someone wanting to kill her.

"I'm twenty-one. I don't need him to be a helicopter parent. You were never like that."

"No one took shots at you until now either," Olivia stated. "He just wants to make sure we're both safe. That's all he's ever wanted."

Why were the men in her life acting like she couldn't take care of herself? She'd done a fair job so far. Why did they think she needed someone to protect her now? Okay, so someone had shot at her, twice. But nothing more had happened since that big truck ran them off the road. That was more than two weeks ago. Maybe the two incidences had nothing to do with each other. She mentally crossed her fingers that it was the truth.

Darrell said he was falling in love with her. It was natural to protect someone you love. But they'd known each other less than a month. Could you really fall in love in a matter of days? She heaved a sigh. Too many things were happening for her to make sense of anything. But she didn't need someone watching her every minute.

Jerrod's sudden attempt at being her big brother was a complete turnaround from that day in the library. What caused the change? Was he trying to lull her into a false sense of security so she would let her guard down? What would he do then? She didn't want Mason's money. Jerrod and Melanie could have it all. If being safe meant signing a paper to that effect, she was willing to do that.

"Honey, despite what you're feeling right now, Mason is still your father and he loves you." Olivia brought her thoughts back to the present. "He's missed out on so much of your life, but he was always there in case we needed something. He's always been there to make sure we were safe. Belinda had far-reaching tentacles, much more than I ever imagined. That's why he stayed in the background of our lives."

"She's gone. She can't hurt us now." Cady shook her head.

"I'm not so sure of that. Look at what Eleanor is saying about Mason."

"But it isn't true, is it? There was nothing online about Belinda's cause of death, but if there had been any question, the police would have arrested him."

"You've been researching him?" One eyebrow arched up.

"Do you blame me? I'd never heard of this guy until your grand announcement that he's my father." There was still a trace of resentment in her voice. "Did he ever tell you how she died?"

"I never asked." Olivia shook her head. "If he was going to kill her, he wouldn't have waited so long. The woman treated all of them terribly. I lived in that house for one school year. It was the worst and the best year of my life. I know without a shadow of a doubt that if he had tried to leave her, she would have done something unthinkable to all of us." She shuddered at the thought. She couldn't help but worry though. Eleanor was saying things that weren't true. How many people will believe the lies?

"Don't forget about Robert," she continued. "The hotel here was supposed to be Jerrod's chance to prove himself to his dad. Yet Belinda and Robert worked against Jerrod to take it away from him. All that mattered to her was hurting Mason. If Jerrod got hurt in the process, she didn't care. Robert is still out there. Until we know whether he is still working to destroy Mason, you could be used to force him to sign over his company. You need to be extra careful until the police figure out who is behind all of this."

Cady's face lost all color and the bees were back in her stomach. Robert had asked her out to get close to her. Was he behind everything that was happening? Why would he kill

Isabell? If he wanted to make Mason look bad in the eyes of the public, he should have been happy about what she was saying about him and Olivia.

She didn't want to believe he would kidnap her, holding her hostage until Mason signed over his company. Was he that desperate? Where was he? Why couldn't the police find him? Did they even consider him a suspect?

Darrell suggested vandalizing her car was more of a juvenile prank than something meant to harm her. Maybe it had nothing to do with Isabell's murder and everything else that was going on. Her head was spinning so fast she couldn't make sense of anything.

"I'll be careful, Mom. I promise. You need to be careful also. After what I saw in the living room last night, I'm not the only one that Mason cares about. You could be used against him as well." A hot blush crept over Olivia's face. She hadn't been aware her daughter had seen the passionate kisses she and Mason had shared the previous evening. She felt like a teenager caught making out with her boyfriend.

"Do you mind?" *Would it matter if she did?* Olivia wondered. She would do anything for her daughter. But Cady would find someone to love soon. Then Olivia would be alone.

Cady thought about it for a minute. Her mom had waited a long time for romance to come back into her life. How could she object? "No." Cady shook her head. "It was sort of embarrassing to see the two of you making out like a couple of teenagers." She giggled. "Kids don't want to think of their parents as sexual beings."

Olivia laughed. "Believe me; parents feel the same way about their kids." She had no idea about Cady's sex life and she wanted to keep it that way. A small shudder shook her trim body.

"I agree that we both need to be careful," she said, getting serious again. "Mason will do anything to protect us. But he

178

can't be everywhere at once."

She paused, looking closely at her daughter. "I have a few questions about what's going on between you and that young deputy." She tipped her head to one side as she looked at her daughter. A red blush had started to spread up her neck to her cheeks. "He seems like a nice young man." A soft smile played around her lips. Cady was still young, but she would love to have grandchildren someday.

Cady shrugged. "I like him. A lot," she added. "We're just feeling our way through this maze right now." She had dated several boys and men while in high school and college. None of them had made her feel what she felt when she was with Darrell. Until they figured out who was doing these things though, romance would have to wait. "I'm not sure whether he's even supposed to be seeing me socially since I could be a suspect in Isabell's murder."

"The police don't consider any of us suspects, do they?" This was one more thing to worry about. She reminded herself that worry didn't help anything. God is in charge of our lives. It was still hard not to worry when the safety of her daughter was at stake. "What would our motive be?" Why kill her after she had exposed Olivia's darkest secret?

Cady shrugged. "Until you mentioned someone could use us to coerce Mason into turning his company over to Robert, I couldn't think of a motive for anyone wanting to hurt me. What are we supposed to do? We can't hide for the rest of our lives."

"No, we can't. But we do need to be careful. Maybe it's a good thing that you're seeing that young deputy." A teasing grin lifted the corners of her mouth when Cady's face turned pink. "I don't think anyone will harm you while you're with him.

179

CHAPTER NINETEEN

Ready to leave for work, Cady remembered she no longer had a car. "I'm going to need a ride to work until I get a rental or get my car back. Even with new tires and windows, I'm not driving it with that stuff painted on the sides." She shook her head. "I can't believe someone would do that."

Olivia held out a key for her.

"What's that?" Cady looked at the key like it might bite her. It wasn't the key to her mom's car.

"Take a look outside." She smiled at her daughter.

A brand new Jeep Wrangler Rubicon was parked in the driveway where her car was usually parked. "Where did that come from?" She turned a suspicious eye on her mom.

Olivia shrugged. "Mason stopped by while you were getting dressed. He thought that was safer than your small compact car. I hate to think what would have happened to the four of you girls if you'd been in your small car when that truck ran you off the road." She shuddered at the thought.

"I don't want him buying me things," Cady said stubbornly. "I have a perfectly good car."

"Really?" Olivia smiled at her. "Where is that car now?"

"You know what I mean. My car is fixable; it's just going to take a few days, maybe a week," she hedged. "When I'm ready for another car, I can buy my own. I don't need him buying things for me. I can't be bought."

She was pacing around the kitchen. "This is exactly why Jerrod was angry when he first came here," she continued. "He called me a gold digger. He and Melanie were afraid I was going to take their inheritance. For all I know they still feel that way and he's just being nice as a cover."

"A cover for what?" Olivia asked, a frown drawing her brows into a V over her pale eyes. "You think maybe he's behind everything that has been happening?" There was a touch of steel in her voice.

"Yes, no, I don't know. All right, so he's done an about-face since he got here, but that could be for show. You didn't see him that day he came into the library. If looks could kill, I wouldn't be standing here talking to you."

Olivia nodded her head. "He's been angry for a long time. His mother had turned him and Melanie against his dad long before I entered the picture. After that, she used us to make them hate him even more. I'm sure she filled their minds with all sorts of horrible things about both of us." A shudder wracked her body as memories of those last weeks in the Jarvis household flooded her mind.

She pushed those thoughts aside. "Since learning what Belinda and Robert were planning, Jerrod has had to reevaluate a lot of things she told him over the years. It's going to take time for him to accept you and me being in his father's life. But I think he's come a long way in a short time. If Mason is going to let Jerrod run this hotel, it's a step in the right direction. Are you willing to try as well?" It sounded like a challenge. She waited to see what Cady would decide.

Cady huffed and puffed for a minute, then nodded her head. "I'll try. I still don't want him buying me a car." She looked out the window. *It is pretty.* She'd always liked Blair's Jeep, she just couldn't afford one. "I'll drive it until my car is fixed. But I'm not keeping it," she said stubbornly. *Maybe,* she silently added.

Darrell stepped out of his big truck as she came outside. "I thought you might need a ride to work this morning, but it looks like you've got that covered." Walking around the candy apple red vehicle, he whistled. "Nice. This belongs to you?" He tipped his head to one side.

"No." She shook her head. "It belongs to Mason. I'm just using it until I get my car back." Something tugged at her heartstrings. She really did like the Jeep.

"Mind if I have a look inside?"

She tossed him the key Mason had left for her. It wasn't the interior he wanted to see though. Opening the driver's door, he popped the hood. "Mighty nice."

Cady looked around his broad shoulders. *Yep, that's an engine,* she thought. All vehicles have them. She didn't know what he was so excited about.

Settling into the soft leather seat, she looked at all the buttons to push. She didn't even know what some of them were for. It would take a week to read the user's manual to figure everything out. Darrell closed the hood and stepped over beside her. Leaning in, he whistled again. "Looks like it's got all the bells and whistles."

Cady sighed. She could get used to this. But she couldn't let herself be caught in the trap. She and her mom had always stood on their own. She didn't want anyone buying her things. Remembering what Olivia had said about the summer trips they'd taken, her tuition paid in full, the money in the bank. Maybe they hadn't been on their own, she decided. What would it hurt to keep the Jeep? She'd have to think about it. Darn. She was already weakening.

Pastor Bryan was waiting when Cady unlocked the door later that morning. This didn't bode well. She sighed. Since her twenty-first birthday, there had been a lot of drama in her life. What else could happen? "Good morning, Pastor. I hope everything is okay?"

"Not exactly." He shook his head. "I heard about your car being vandalized last night."

"Bad news travels fast," Cady sighed.

"That it does. I've also heard what Eleanor is saying about Mr. Jarvis. I tried having a talk with her. Needless to say, it didn't go very well. She is convinced she's doing God's work by exposing a killer."

"Mason didn't kill his wife," she whispered harshly unconsciously defending him. Standing up, she moved to a more secluded spot. Several others had come in when Pastor Bryan had. They were already taking note of their whispered conversation. She didn't want to add to the gossip that Eleanor was already spreading around. The Bible says the tongue is like a wildfire that needs to be tamed. She was sure gossip is what was being referred to. "There is nothing online to suggest that he killed his wife."

"I'm sure you're right, but I wanted to give you a heads up. Mr. Jarvis might want to contact a lawyer."

"That would make him look guilty, like he has something to hide."

He nodded his head. "I'm afraid it's a Catch 22 for him. He needs to protect himself though. Eleanor is on a crusade to 'rid the world of all cheaters'. Her words, not mine. She hasn't been able to get past what her husband did," he said, confirming what Martha had told her. "Each time there is something on the news about a high-powered man cheating on his wife, it gets worse, I'm afraid." He shook his head sadly.

"I don't know how Isabell managed to dig up what happened between Mr. Jarvis and your mom," he continued. "But it brought all of the bad memories back for Eleanor. I will keep trying to talk some sense into her, but I'm afraid it might be too late. She is seeing conspiracies everywhere. She accused me of siding with Satan." He gave a tired sigh. "She needs more help than I can give her. It's up to God to straighten out her mind and her heart. I just thought you should know."

"Thanks, Pastor. Do you think she vandalized my car?"

He shrugged. "It's a possibility. The police might want to talk to her." He turned to leave.

Something he'd said stuck in her mind. How had Isabell found out that Mason was her father? To the best of her knowledge, only four people in town knew: Mason, Olivia, Jerrod, and Cady. No, there was more than that. She'd told Blair and Darrell. Robert also knew about that particular skeleton in her closet. That meant one of those was working an agenda where telling Isabell would help.

If Eleanor began spouting her conspiracy that Mason had killed Belinda, what would the sheriff do? Contacting the police in San Francisco would only make things worse for Mason. Innocent people were convicted of crimes they didn't commit all the time. She didn't want that to happen to him.

The deputy who had taken the report about her car the night before stopped by mid-morning. Library patrons stopped what they were doing to watch what was going to happen next. This was better than any soap opera on television.

"The forensic techs were able to pull several usable prints off your car, but as expected most of them were yours." He shrugged. "Were you able to think of anyone else with a grudge against you?"

He'd asked her that when he took the report. She looked down at the floor, her dark hair falling forward shielding her face from his scrutiny. Absently brushing it out of her face, she debated whether to say anything about the pastor's visit. She shook her head. "I'm sorry, I'm sure I've managed to tick people off at some time, but I can't think of anyone that would do this."

He had heard what Eleanor was saying, what Isabell had said. By now everyone in town knew Mason was her father. It was only natural for him to connect the dots. Without any evidence, there was no way to prove who had vandalized her car. No matter, she wasn't going to point fingers. That would make her no better than Isabell and Eleanor.

"Okay, you have my card. If you think of anyone besides Robert Gaston and Eleanor Davis, give me a call. You can have your insurance company repair your car now. There's no evidence we can use to find the suspect." He walked out shaking his head.

~~~

Darrell was working late, but he promised to stop by when he got off shift. That meant Cady was stuck with having dinner with Mason and Jerrod. She was getting used to Mason, but Jerrod was beginning to get on her nerves. He seemed to enjoy tormenting her. Was that what older brothers did to their younger sisters? Was this what she had to look forward to since he was moving to Tumbleweed? She wasn't sure if the General Manager of a hotel lived in a suite at the hotel or if he had an apartment.

Mason pulled into the drive as she was getting out of the Jeep. *Is Jerrod going to make it a habit to be here every night for dinner?* she wondered. *How long is Mason planning on being here?* She didn't have any answers.

"Nice Jeep." Jerrod looked it over much like Darrell had that morning.

"Yes, it is," she stated noncommittally. "My car won't be ready for me to drive for a few more days. Your dad…"

"Our dad," he interrupted, correcting her.

Glaring at him, she went on as though he hadn't said anything. "… got this for me to use until my car is ready."

"It's yours, Cady," Mason stopped beside them. "Don't you like it? You can pick out a different color if you'd rather have something else. I just thought this would be safer than your compact car."

"Thank you, but I don't need you to do that. I'll drive it until my car is repainted."

"Suit yourself." He turned away but not before she saw the hurt on his face.

"You really can be a jerk sometimes, you know that? I guess that proves we are related." He shook his head. "He's trying to be nice. Maybe you could try that, too." Jerrod

185

headed for the house.

"Are you admitting that you're a jerk?" Grabbing her purse and book bag, she hustled after him.

"Sometimes, yeah, I'm a jerk. I'm working on improving that. How about giving it a try?" He looked down at her. Still squabbling when they walked into the kitchen, she stopped just inside the door. "What?" There was a goofy grin on her mom's face.

"Nothing." Olivia shook her head. Her expression was a little too innocent for that to be anything but a lie.

"I'm going upstairs to change." Olivia's laughter followed her as she stomped up the back stairs. Taking her time changing out of her dress slacks and blouse, she tried to figure out what her mom found so funny about her and Jerrod arguing. *Shouldn't she be upset with me?* She had expected her mom to be mad at her.

Being an only child, she never had anyone to argue with besides her mom. Blair on the other hand had two older brothers. Remembering how they had argued when they were teenagers, she sighed. Olivia probably thought she and Jerrod were beginning to act like siblings. "Heaven help me," she grumbled as she marched back to the kitchen.

CHAPTER TWENTY

"I had a visit from a deputy this morning," Mason was saying as Cady walked in. "It seems Eleanor Davis paid a visit to the sheriff claiming to have inside information about Belinda's death. Or as she called it, about her murder." He sighed.

"I was out of town when she died as were Jerrod and Melanie," he went on. "Belinda was home alone when she died. None of us were aware she had fired her latest nurse that day. According to the coroner's report, her blood-alcohol level was almost three times the legal limit. She fell down the stairs. There was a full bottle of bourbon beside her on the stairs. The coroner estimated she had been dead more than twelve hours when the housekeeper found her."

Cady stepped further into the room. "Why did she have a nurse? Was she sick?"

"Only if you consider being as mean as a snake being sick," Jerrod answered before Mason could say anything. "Since alcoholism is a recognized disease, I guess you could say she was sick. She was a mean, falling down drunk."

"That's enough, Jerrod," Mason said gently. "She was still your mother."

"A very poor excuse for a mother," Jerrod argued. He didn't attempt to hide the contempt he felt for her. He pushed back from the table to pace across the room. After finding out what Belinda had tried to do to him, Cady couldn't blame him for being angry. His feelings of betrayal went far beyond what Cady felt after learning about Mason.

"Yes, she was an alcoholic," Mason confirmed. "Her liver was failing because of years of drinking. The doctors said a transplant wouldn't help since she refused to quit. I had hired nurses for the past few years to be with her while I was gone.

It never did any good. She fired them as fast as I hired them." He ran his long fingers through his hair making it stand up.

"If I had known about the plan she and Robert had going…" He shook his head. "That might have given me the motive to do what Eleanor says I did. But I had no idea what they were up to until I arrived here."

His voice had taken on a faraway quality as though he was looking back on his life. "I wish I could do things over, but I can't. All I can do now is try to mend things with all three of my children. And with you," he added, looking at Olivia. "I am truly sorry for how I screwed up."

Jerrod nodded his head, accepting his dad's apology. Unsure what to say, Cady settled for tipping her head slightly in acknowledgment of his words.

Sometime during this narration, Olivia had taken his hand. Cady said a small prayer that this would all be over soon. She wanted her mom to be happy. If that meant Mason was part of their lives, she could live with that.

Before the silence could get maudlin, Mason cleared his throat and continued. "I gave the deputy the doctor's name as well as the nurse Belinda had fired that day. Dr. McCloud had been treating Belinda for quite a few years. He'll confirm her medical condition.

"I also gave him the list of hotels where I was working that week. They were all on the east coast. There are plenty of people who can confirm that I was there. I couldn't have made it to San Francisco and back without someone noticing my absence."

"The day she died, I was here in Tumbleweed checking up on the finishing touches to the construction," Jerrod added, shaking his head. "Knowing what I know now, I realize how stupid I've been. Robert was heading up the construction end and planning on taking over as manager when the hotel was finished. He even helped pick out the site.

"I wasn't here throughout construction, but when I did come to check on things, I flew into Flagstaff and rented a car. Since Robert had an apartment, I stayed with him. Few people even knew a Jarvis was in town. Robert said it was better that way. Now I know why." He looked at Olivia. "I had no idea this is where you and Cady were living. But Mother knew. Apparently, she wanted to spring this takeover on everyone once it was a done deal. I think it was her way of saying she was better than the rest of us." He shrugged his broad shoulders.

"It's not your fault, Son." Mason rested his hand on Jerrod's shoulder. "I wasn't any wiser to their plans than you were. I was trying to give you space to show what you could do, or I would have been here to oversee what was going on."

He drew a deep breath. "Besides, coming here without seeing Olivia and Cady would have been impossible for me. I kept hoping Belinda would eventually stop threatening to harm them, but that never happened. After she was gone, I saw it as an opportunity to get to know my second daughter." He looked at Cady. "I know I shouldn't have just popped into your life the way I did. Again, I'm sorry for how I've handled everything. I hope you can forgive me someday."

"Make my mom happy and we'll be fine," she whispered. His explanation for waiting until now to come forward was making sense. She could accept it.

"I'll do my best to make her happy," Mason assured her.

Turning back to Jerrod, he asked, "Did you see the blueprints for the hotel before they began construction?" Jerrod had taken architectural engineering in college. He should have seen the difference between this hotel and the other properties in the Jarvis House chain.

"Yeah, but the ones I saw aren't what the building looks like now. They must have had two sets of blueprints. Mother kept me busy picking out furnishings for the rooms during the

189

final months of construction. I didn't see the final results until I was in town for the grand opening." A muscle in his jaw bunched up. "When I confronted Robert, he said the town fathers hadn't approved of the original plans. He said he was sure he told me about the changes. I'm just as sure he didn't."

During dinner, they talked about their day instead of less pleasant matters. Hopefully, once the sheriff talked to Belinda's doctor and nurse, Eleanor's rumors could be put to rest once and for all. But Cady knew it was easier to start rumors than it was to stop them.

It was after nine when Darrell finally got off work. "Sorry to stop by this late." He looked at Cady. "There was an accident on the highway. I was tied up longer than I'd expected."

"Have you had dinner yet?" Cady asked.

"No, I was hoping you'd join me for dessert while I ate." Her heart fluttered at the look in his eyes.

"There are plenty of leftovers in the refrigerator," Olivia said. "It will only take a few minutes to heat them. I hope you like Cajun Alfredo chicken."

"Never had it, but it sounds great. I don't want to put you out though."

"You aren't putting anyone out. Go relax on the porch. I'll bring a big bowl right out. No one had room for the pie I had for dessert after dinner. Maybe now is a good time?" She looked at the others.

Mason groaned. "I'm going to gain fifty pounds if I keep eating like this but I'm not one to pass up pie. I'll help you in the kitchen."

When Jerrod followed Cady and Darrell out to the porch, she glared at him. "Where are you going?"

"It's a nice night. I thought I'd join you on the porch." He ignored the stink eye Cady sent in his direction.

Taking Cady's hand, Darrell chuckled. He remembered

similar looks from his younger sister when she was dating the man she eventually married. Cady might not want to admit it, but they were acting like siblings.

Only minutes later, Mason brought out a tray laden with food. Olivia was behind him with a pot of coffee. "It's decaf," she said, holding up the pot. "I didn't want to keep everyone up with regular, but pie is always good with coffee."

For a while, they were able to put aside all the problems plaguing them. *Was this how life would have been if Mason had taken Jerrod and Melanie and married her mom?* Cady looked up at the night sky. The stars looked like diamonds on a black velvet cloth.

When a yawn caught Darrell by surprise, he stood up. "I guess I'd better get going. I'm on duty early tomorrow." He looked at Olivia. "Thank you for dinner. I didn't expect you to feed me, but it was delicious." He held out his hand to Cady.

She gladly placed her hand in his. "I'm surprised you remembered I was here," she teased when they were finally alone. "You seem to have hit it off with Mason and Jerrod."

Darrell nodded his head. "Yeah, I like them. I hope you do too. I think they're both planning on sticking around."

She sighed. "That's what it looks like."

"Do you mind?" He tipped his head so he could look down at her.

"No, I guess not." She shook her head. "The shock of learning I have a father and brother is beginning to wear off. I hope meeting my sister isn't as traumatic as this has been." She sighed. "I suppose you've heard the latest gossip?" Would he be able to tell her if the sheriff had talked to the detective in San Francisco about Belinda's death?

"It's pretty hard to miss. I'm surprised Mrs. Davis hasn't called a news conference to announce what she believes. The sheriff warned her that she could get in a heap of trouble, but she isn't interested in hearing the truth. Sheriff Taylor talked to the detective in San Francisco who investigated Belinda Jarvis' death. There isn't a shred of truth to what she's saying. That doesn't mean people will hear that part of the conversation."

Placing a light kiss on her lips, he changed the subject. "The evening didn't turn out quite the way I'd planned," he chuckled. He didn't give her a chance to answer as he pulled her closer. When another yawn snuck up on him, he sighed. "I'm sorry. I've been up since four this morning and my shift starts again at seven tomorrow."

"Why did you get up so early if your shift didn't start until seven?"

"It's easier to work out before going to work than after." He shrugged. "It's a routine I started when I was a teenager and it carried over into the military. It's a habit now. I'll try to do better this weekend. I managed to get a day off then. Are you up for a hike?"

"You bet." She smiled happily. "There are still a lot of trails I haven't shown you."

It was several more minutes before he finally got in his truck. "I'll see you tomorrow. Hopefully, it won't be as late. Dinner will be on me." He leaned out the window for one last kiss.

Cady stayed outside watching the taillights on his truck disappeared into the dark before wandering back inside.

CHAPTER TWENTY-ONE

Leaving work the next day, there was a note under the windshield wiper of the Jeep. Looking around, there was no one else in the parking lot. Martha had left several minutes ahead of Cady. If she'd forgotten something, it would be faster to go back inside than try to find a paper and pen to write a note.

Butterflies fluttered in her stomach as she pulled the single piece of paper from under the wiper blade and unfolded it. The scrawled writing was hard to read.

Miss Cady. I know who killed that mean lady. Meet me behind the big hotel where they found her. I'm afraid to call the police. Thanks, Henry.

She reread the note three times trying to make sense of it. Why would Henry tell her instead of calling the police? Living on the street made people cautious even of the police. Was that why he was afraid to call them? How had he discovered who killed Isabell? Debating the wisdom of doing what he asked, she stepped up into the high Jeep.

Darrell would be picking her up for dinner in an hour and a half. That gave her time to meet Henry at the hotel. Hopefully, she could convince him to let her call Darrell. If this took too long, she'd send him a text to let him know she might be a few minutes late.

The alley behind the Jarvis House Hotel where the dumpsters were kept was shrouded with shadows when she pulled up. There was no one around. Had Henry decided not to meet her? Had something scared him off? It hadn't occurred to her to wonder why he wanted to meet her here until now.

Seeing movement out of the corner of her eye, she jerked around to see a figure approaching the Jeep. Her heart was in her throat. His hoodie was pulled low over his face. "Henry?"

Her voice wobbled. The window was only down a few inches and she wasn't sure he heard her. She breathed a sigh of relief when he pushed the hood back so she could see his face.

"Henry, what are you doing here? You said you know who killed Isabell. You need to call the police." The words tumbled out before she could stop them.

He shook his head. "No, I can't do that, Miss Cady." His eyes roamed over the area like he thought someone was going to jump out at him. "You didn't tell nobody about me, did you?"

She frowned. "I have a date tonight," she improvised. "I had to let him know I was running late." A flash of anger crossed his weathered features. It was gone so fast, Cady wasn't sure she'd seen anything.

He reached for the door handle. "Unlock the door so I can get in." He tugged at the handle. "Nobody can see me standing out here like this."

"What's going on, Henry? Why did you leave me that note? Do you know who killed Isabell?" The flutter in her stomach said there was something wrong with this scenario.

"I'd never lie to you, Miss Cady. I just gotta show you what I found in the dumpster. Please unlock the door."

"You found something in the dumpster?" She was confused. "You said you know who killed her."

"Hurry up and unlock the door." His tone changed from pleading to demanding. He quickly scanned the area to make sure no one was watching them. "What I got to show you will prove he killed her."

"He who? Why are you showing me instead of the sheriff?"

He gave his head a shake. "Cops don't like homeless folks. They'll say I killed her and put me in jail. You don't want me to go to jail, do you, Miss Cady. I thought you were my friend." His faded eyes grew misty.

"Yes, I am your friend." Giving in, she sighed, releasing the lock on the door. Henry scurried around to the passenger side of the Jeep. Her pulse quickened as he climbed in beside her. Was it a huge mistake coming here alone? "I know they'll believe you. Your boyfriend is a deputy, isn't he?"

"Um, yes, Darrell is a deputy. You need to let me call him if you know who killed Isabell."

"Noooo," he wailed. "You can't do that to me."

"Okay. Tell me what you know. I'll tell the police, but they aren't going to take my word for it. If you know something, you need to tell them."

He started shaking his head. "No, I can't do that." There was a touch of panic in his voice. He'd always seemed so comfortable with who he is. Why this sudden uncertainty?

Something occurred to her, and a frown drew her brows down over her eyes. "How did you know this was my vehicle? I didn't have the Jeep when you were still staying at the library." Looking at him, suspicion clouded her eyes.

"I've been looking out for you, just like I did when I was staying behind that dumpster. I didn't want someone to hurt you. I saw what that man did to your pretty little car, too. He shouldn't have done that. That's why I left that note. I knew you'd stop him from hurting anyone else." He was pushing that point a little too hard.

"Who did you see?"

"That man, the one that killed the mean lady."

"What man?" She was getting frustrated when he wouldn't tell her who he meant. "Tell me what you know, and I'll tell Darrell. I'll make sure he won't arrest you." He'd been eager to get in the Jeep with her, but now he was dragging his feet. Why was he stalling if he really had something to say?

"It was that big man that came to your house," he finally answered. It didn't occur to her to ask how he knew about someone coming to her house.

The swarm of bees was back in Cady's stomach. "Do you mean Mason or Jerrod Jarvis? You saw one of them kill Isabell?" There was a huge gap in his story that wasn't making sense.

His head bobbed up and down. "It was the old man. I saw him put her in that dumpster."

"You're saying Mason Jarvis put Isabell's body in the dumpster?"

His head bobbed up and down again. He was beginning to look like a bobble head doll. "I did." His eyes were big in his whiskered face.

"How did you see him? Where were you when you saw this?"

"After that mean lady chased me away from the library, I needed to find another place to stay. Fancy places like this hotel always throw out lots of food. I came here to find something to eat before I looked for my next camp spot. I was going through the dumpster when this fancy car pulled up. I hid before that man could see me. He took her body out of the trunk and just tossed her away like she was garbage."

"Why didn't you tell someone before this? It's been more than a week since she was killed." She was careful not to let on that she was beginning to doubt his story. She didn't know why he would make up something like this though. The sheriff's department had gone through the security videos. Neither Mason nor Jerrod had left their suite that night.

"See, even you don't believe me, and we were friends." He looked down at his lap. "Why would the cops believe me when you don't? They'd say I killed her."

Before she could make sense of this, someone tapped on the window beside her head. Whiling around, she recoiled at the sight of the business end of a gun pointed at her through the window. "Wh...what's going on?" She turned to stare at Henry. Why hadn't he warned her that someone was approaching the Jeep? He was cowering between the seat and the door. He wasn't going to be any help.

Her eyes trailed up from the hand holding the gun to the face hidden by the hoodie. "Not again with the hoodie," she muttered. "What's going on?" Her voice was sharp with frustration. Probably not the smartest tone to use when someone is pointing a gun at you. But she couldn't help it.

"Shut off the engine and get out," the man in the hoodie growled at her. "You too old man."

For a brief moment, Cady stared at him. She recognized the voice. This time she was smart enough to keep her mouth shut. "I said turn the car off and get out. Now," he barked.

Expecting her to be intimidated, he wasn't prepared for her to give the door a hard shove. He staggered back several steps but recovered before Cady could close the door again. "That wasn't a smart move," he growled. The hood started to slip, and he quickly pulled it forward again. He wasn't aware she'd recognized his voice and wasn't ready to reveal his identity yet.

Gripping her arm, he dragged her out of the Jeep. His fingers dug into her arm hard enough to leave bruises. She grimaced but refused to cry out. There wasn't anyone around to hear her anyway.

"You heard me, old man. Get out. You're coming with me."

"D...don't hurt me," Henry stammered. "I ain't done nothing wrong."

Cady gave him a curious look. She hadn't taken him for the type to cower in the face of a bully. There was something wrong with this whole scene. Maybe he was giving their captor a false sense of being in charge.

"Why are you doing this? What do you want with me?" Cady tried to drag her feet, but he was having none of it. He spun her around getting in her face. "Unless you want me to end this right here, you'll do as you're told. Now, get moving."

"Fine," she huffed. "Where are you taking me? My father owns this hotel."

"Not for long." The answer came from inside the hoodie. If she hadn't already known his identity, this would have given him away. "You're coming with me," he added.

"Where are you taking me?" Her heart was in her throat making it hard to breathe. A hostage only stayed alive as long as they were useful. After that, they became a liability. She had to do something before that happened. She had to do something fast. How had she been so stupid not to tell anyone she was coming here? She prayed that the security cameras on the back of the building were working now.

She looked over her shoulder to see what Henry was doing? Was he part of this? Her head swiveled around. "Where's Henry?" He'd managed to escape into the shadows.

"Don't worry about him." Her abductor tugged on her arm again as he dragged her toward a commercial van she hadn't noticed before. Pushing her against the side of the van, he twisted her arm behind her back. Feeling something circle her wrist, she began to struggle. "No. I'm not going to go quietly to my death. Help!" Her voice rose to a high-pitched shriek.

"You bitch." Grabbing her hair, he pulled her head back so far she thought he was trying to snap her neck. Slamming her head against the side of the van, she saw stars for a second before everything went black.

When she opened her eyes again, her hands were secured behind her back. She was lying in the back of the van. She could feel it moving. How long had she been out? Where was he taking her? How long before someone realized she was missing?

She'd been talking to Henry for a while before the gunman appeared. It had to be after six by now. Darrell would be at the house soon to pick her up. Would they realize she was in trouble? How would they find out where he was taking her? The thoughts swirling around in her mind caused her head to hurt.

It was only minutes before she felt the van shift gears and bounce over a curb somewhere. Closing her eyes so her abductor wouldn't know she was awake, she didn't resist when he pulled on her feet. He'd made the mistake of not binding her feet together as well as her hands. If she could surprise him, she might be able to escape. If they were in the forest, she would have an advantage. She knew every trail but her abductor didn't.

Waiting for an opportunity, she watched him through her eyelashes. As her backside cleared the edge of the van, she kicked him in the head. He fell to the broken pavement, and Cady slid the rest of the way out of the van. The instant her feet hit the ground, she started running.

"Stop right there, or I'll shoot you in the back." Before she was less than five feet away, he recovered enough to pull the gun from the pocket of his hoodie. Would he really shoot her? Was she willing to risk it? She stumbled to a stop. Frustrated tears blurred her vision as he pulled her toward a building.

"Where are we?" Looking around, she recognized the rundown motel at the edge of town. The town council had been trying to get the owners to either fix the place up or tear it down. "What are you planning on doing?"

"Exactly what I started to do when I came here," he growled. Hiding his identity was no longer necessary, and he pushed the hood off his head.

Cady tried to remain calm in the face of the anger and hatred she saw on his face. "Why do you need me? What are you going to do to me?" Her heart was pounding so hard she thought it was going to jump out of her chest.

"Don't try any more tricks and you won't get hurt. You're

199

just a pawn in a real-life game of chess. Shall we see what daddy dearest's next move will be? How much do you think he cares about you?" She resisted his effort to pull her toward the building. "Everything Jarvis owns is going to belong to me."

"How do you figure that?" If he was planning on using her to force Mason to sign over his company, it would only work if they both ended up dead.

"Jarvis stole my grandpa's company. I'm taking back what is rightfully mine."

"How do you figure it should be yours?" As long as they were talking, she was still alive. "Mason paid his father-in-law for the company," she argued.

"Not what it was worth."

"It wasn't worth much when your grandpa owned it." She looked around. "It was just two motels not much better than this place. Mason turned it into something worth a lot of money."

"Money that should be mine," Robert growled, giving her arm a shake. "If he hadn't stolen those motels from my grandpa, I would have turned them into something better. I never got that chance."

Using a key card he pulled out of the pocket of his hoodie, he pushed the door open. Releasing her arm, he shoved her inside and slammed the door behind him.

She stumbled across the room, catching herself on the edge of a messy bed. She turned to face him defiantly. "What do you think kidnapping me is going to accomplish? Forcing Mason to turn over the company won't hold up in a court of law. In case you aren't aware, extortion is illegal." She couldn't seem to stop herself from taunting him.

"Just shut up. I need to think." He paced in front of the door. This wasn't going the way he'd planned. Nothing was going the way he'd planned. If Belinda hadn't drunk herself into a stupor, this would have worked out.

"Where did Henry go? Is he part of your plan? Did you pay him to be my friend?"

"I said to sit down and shut up. I have to think." He took a menacing step toward her.

When she didn't obey immediately, he growled at her. "Sit. Down."

She sank down on the edge of the bed only to bounce back up. She didn't know what kind of bugs were crawling around in those dirty sheets. Didn't the motel even offer maid service?

At a knock on the door, he whirled around. His eyes were wild now. He was completely unhinged. Pulling the gun from his pocket, he cautiously approached the door. "Who's there?"

"Who the hell do you think? Now open up." The muffled voice came through the thin door.

Robert opened the door a crack but kept the chain lock in place. "What are you doing here?" he whispered. "I thought you were going to stay out of sight for a while."

"I changed my mind. Now, open the damned door." He pushed on the door causing the chain to strain the screws attaching it to the door.

Robert obediently did as he was told, releasing the chain lock and stepping back. Before closing the door again, he looked outside to make sure there wasn't anyone else around. "What are you doing here?"

He ignored Robert's question "I ditched that fancy Jeep her daddy bought her. The thing probably has GPS. Can't have them finding her before we're ready. Go outside and keep an eye on things. I don't want anyone showing up until I'm ready."

Turning to Cady, the man swept his hand across his body, bending low in a mock bow. "How has my grandson been treating you, Miss Cady?" He gave a loud guffaw. "I see you've finally put the pieces together. I thought you were smarter than that." A sneer curled his lips. "Knowing what that bastard and your mama did to my daughter, I about got sick every time I had to be nice to you."

"Did you kill Isabell? Why would you do that? She was telling people about my mom and Mason. Wasn't that why you told her about us?"

He shrugged. "I didn't tell her. Mason Jarvis killed her to keep her quiet. That other woman is also causing him quite a bit of trouble now. He'll kill her to silence her, too." His laugh was almost maniacal.

"Why are you doing this? Don't you care that you're hurting Jerrod and Melanie, too? They're your grandchildren, the same as Robert."

He glared at her. "They're the spawn of that devil Jarvis. He cheated me out of my company. When I wanted back in with him, he wouldn't even give me my fair share."

"You gave those motels to Mason as a wedding present, but he still paid you for them. He turned them in to something to be proud of." She tried to keep her voice reasonable.

"Wedding present, ha. My little girl loved him and he cheated on her with your mama. You know what that makes you?" He leaned over, getting in her face.

"Yes, I know what that makes me." She stiffened her spine, drawing herself up to close to his height. "It makes me very glad I'm not your granddaughter."

He backhanded her, sending her to the floor so quickly she didn't have time to duck. Blood trickled down her chin from her split lip. Stars flashed before her eyes and she shook them away. *Please, God. Don't let me pass out again.* She didn't know what he would do to her if she couldn't fight back.

"You need to learn some manners, Missy. It's time for you to shut your mouth. I got business to take care of."

Stepping over her prone form, he lifted her off the floor like she was a rag doll. The man was stronger than he looked.

Throwing her into the one chair in the room, he secured her already bound hands to the chair.

"What are you going to do to me?"

"I said to shut your mouth. When I'm ready for you to say something, I'll tell you what to say." He went into the bathroom, slamming the door behind him. Within seconds, she heard the toilet flush and the shower turned on.

Sighing with relief, Cady looked around for some way to break the bonds that tied her to the chair. Anything that would make noise was out. Even with the shower water running, he would be able to hear if she started rocking the chair back and forth. She didn't have long to come up with some way to escape.

When the outside door burst open, slamming into the wall, her heart nearly stopped. Robert pushed Eleanor ahead of him into the room. "Cady. Are you all right?" The older woman started across the room only to be stopped by Robert's firm grip on her arm.

"Not so fast, old woman." He jerked her back. "Gramps, where are you?" His eyes were wild as he looked around. He obviously wasn't in the small room.

The shower water shut off and seconds later Henry pulled open the bathroom door. Eleanor gasped. "For all that's holy, man, at least wrap a towel around your waist." She placed her free hand at her waist as though ordering Henry to obey her command.

Cady said a prayer of thanks that she had her back to the bathroom. Seeing Henry's naked body was something she'd never be able to scrub from her mind.

"Shut up," Henry snapped. He didn't bother to grab a towel. "What's going on?" He glared at his grandson.

"I found her sneaking around outside," Robert said. "It's that other woman you told about Jarvis. What should I do with her?" He waited for directions.

"Grrr," Henry growled, swiping at the shampoo oozing down his forehead into his eyes. "Find something to tie her up with. Then get back outside to make sure there isn't anyone else snooping around. I need to finish my shower." With that, the bathroom door slammed shut again.

When Robert pushed Eleanor down onto the bed, she immediately bounced back up. "Don't think for a second that I'm going to let you rape me on this filthy bed." *As opposed to a clean bed,* Cady thought.

"Rape you," Robert squawked. "I'd rather die first. Turn around." Grabbing her arm, he twisted her so her back was to him. He pulled another zip tie out of his pocket, securing her hands. There were no more chairs in the room. Since she didn't want to sit on the bed, he pushed her to the floor. "Is that better?" he asked her mockingly.

"I'd rather stand," she stated haughtily. She struggled to stand up, but he pushed her back to the floor.

"Stay." It sounded like he was speaking to a dog. She huffed and puffed, but stayed on the floor as ordered. Seeing that she didn't try to get up again, he went back outside as his grandpa ordered.

CHAPTER TWENTY-TWO

"Cady, what's going on? Who are these men?" Once Robert was outside Eleanor scooted around so she was facing Cady.

"That man," she tipped her head toward the door, "is Robert Gaston. He was the manager at the Jarvis House Hotel until Mason fired him. The old man is his grandpa. They want to force Mason to sign over his company to them."

"Why would Mr. Jarvis do that?" she asked indignantly.

Not even Eleanor knew the history of this crazy family, and that was a good thing. But there wasn't time to explain now. "Can you scoot over here and untie me? We need to get loose."

"This carpet is filthy," the older woman said with her nose in the air. "It's bad enough to be forced to sit here without scooting on it. I'll never be able to get my clothes clean."

"Oh, for heaven's sake, Eleanor," Cady sighed. "What is more important, keeping your clothes clean or escaping these two lunatics? Henry isn't going to take forever in the shower."

"Well, when you put it like that," she huffed and began scooting toward Cady. "I can't reach your hands," Eleanor whined. "What am I supposed to do? My hands are tied, too, you know."

"Do something before it's too late." The shower turned off as she spoke. "Hurry up," Cady urged. She couldn't decide what was more difficult; getting the knots out of the rope holding her to the chair, or getting Eleanor to do something. She could feel her fumbling with the ropes when the bathroom door opened. *Damn.*

"Oh, for the love of Pete," Henry mumbled. Without bothering to let Eleanor stand up, he dragged her away from Cady on her knees.

"Ow, ow, ow," she wailed. "I'm getting rug burns." Tears traveled down her cheeks.

Cady was thankful that he had on a pair of wrinkled pants when she peeked through her lashes at him. His sagging chest was bare, but that she could live with. "What are you going to do with us now?" she asked.

"Now, the negotiations begin," he stated, pulling a cell phone out of his pants pocket. "Hello, Jarvis, this is Henry," he said when Mason answered the phone. "You know; your father-in-law."

"What have you done to my daughter?" Even though Henry didn't have the phone on speaker, Cady could hear Mason shout at the older man.

"Nothing yet, but that depends on you. Come to the Day Break Motel at the edge of town. We'll see how things go from there. Come alone. You have a half-hour." He disconnected the call. Turning, he looked down at Eleanor. "You don't have any negotiating value to me. What should I do with you?"

Eleanor stared at him defiantly without saying a word.

"I suppose Jarvis will be glad to have you out of his hair." Gripping her arm, he hauled her to her feet. "If you'll stay real quiet," he placed his finger over her lips, "I might let you live. Can you do that for me?"

Her eyes were big in her face and she nodded her head. "Good." He led her into the bathroom. A loud thud was followed by a groan and another thud as Eleanor fell to the floor.

The sound of tires crunching on the gravel parking lot and headlights flashing across the window said they had company. Henry rubbed his hands together. He was going to enjoy putting Jarvis in his place. Once he had the big man's signature on the dotted line, he was going to pay the ultimate price for what he'd done to Belinda.

Robert pushed Mason into the room. "I frisked him. He isn't armed," he informed his grandpa importantly.

"Well, it didn't take you long to get here." Henry stopped Mason when he started to rush to Cady. "Not so fast. We got some talking to do before I let you near her. Have a seat right there on the bed. Sorry about the mess, but maid service here isn't what you're used to at my hotels."

"Those are my hotels," Mason corrected him.

"Not for long if you don't want this one getting hurt." He pointed at Cady.

Mason's face lost all color. "You'd kill an innocent girl over a bunch of hotels?"

"I'd kill a room full of innocent girls if it meant getting back what you took from me. But the one thing I can't get back is my daughter. You took her away, and now she's dead. You took my daughter, I'll take yours. Seems fair to me."

"You bastard." Mason would have jumped on the old man if Robert hadn't hit him with the gun he was still holding.

Cady gasped and jerked against her restraints. There was nothing she could do though.

"Now that I have your attention, let's talk business." Henry leaned against the wall next to the window. All eyes turned to the door when someone pushed it open. "What the..." Henry stopped, staring at the person standing in the doorway. "Belinda? You're back. They told me you were dead." Tears sparkled in his faded eyes, running down his cheeks.

"Yes, I'm back," she answered haughtily. She marched across the room with the regal manner of a queen inspecting her subjects. No one said anything while she moved around the small room. Cady couldn't judge her expression when she paused in front of Mason. A frown creased his forehead, but he didn't say anything to her. Was he seeing his daughter? Or was he under the same illusion as Henry that his dead wife was back from the grave?

There was little doubt in Cady's mind that this was her half-sister Melanie. With the same white-blonde hair and startling blue eyes as Jerrod, there was little doubt the two were related. Mason had said she was the image of her mother, inside and out. That didn't bode well for what came next. There was no telling what she brought to this game of chess Henry was playing.

For a long moment, the woman stopped to study Cady. There was no expression on her face, leaving Cady to guess at her thoughts. Giving a slight nod, she whirled around to look at the two men across the room. When she finally broke the silence, there was the same haughty tone Cady imagined royalty used when they were speaking to lesser beings. "Would one of you like to explain to me what's going on here?"

Robert approached his grandpa, whispering in his ear. Henry looked confused for a minute as he stared at the woman standing across from him. "Belinda? Melanie?" he whispered.

She shrugged. "Either one will do. Mother always told me I was her double. I was destined to take her place."

Still unable to decide who he was looking at Henry remained at a loss for words. "Well, speak up," she demanded. "Tell me what you're doing here. You aren't trying to take my company away from me, are you?" Her manner was so regal Cady could imagine a crown on her white-blonde head.

"No, no, I would never do that to you. You and Robert can have the company. It's your birthright."

Robert started to sputter, but Henry silenced him with a look.

"And what about Jerrod?" she asked mildly. "Doesn't he have a birthright as well?" She was pacing between Henry and her father. "After all, he is the son of the almighty Belinda." Henry missed the scorn in her voice.

"Oh, sure, sure," Henry quickly agreed. "It's only fair." Robert continued to sputter, but no one was paying any attention to him. All eyes were focused on Melanie.

At a sudden shriek from the bathroom, everyone turned to the closed door. The bathroom door crashed open, at the same time the outside door burst open. "Don't anyone move and keep your hands where they can be seen," Sheriff Taylor shouted. The small room was suddenly crowded with men pointing guns at Robert and Henry.

A deputy helped a slightly disoriented Eleanor out of the bathroom. There was a large lump on the side of her head where Henry had knocked her out. She sank down onto the chair Cady had vacated when Darrell cut her free. "What's going on? I don't feel so good."

"It took you long enough," Mason growled. "What were you waiting for?" He looked between his daughters. Darrell was holding Cady like he was never going to let go. He approached Melanie cautiously, unsure what side she was on.

"Aren't you glad to see me, father?" she asked in the same haughty tone. Her lips twitched slightly.

"Um, of course, but..." He stopped unsure what to say next, finally asking, "What are you doing here? I thought you were still in rehab."

"I was." She nodded. "After you called to check on me, I knew something bad had happened. I knew these two were behind it." She looked at her cousin and grandpa. The deputies had them handcuffed and they were sitting on the floor against the wall. She looked down at her grandpa. "Did you really think Belinda could come back from the dead?" Her voice dripped with disdain. She'd stopped thinking of the woman who'd given her life as her mother a long time ago. "Even she couldn't do that."

Henry hung his head, a single tear trailed down his withered face.

"Did you know she hated you as much as she hated the rest of us?" she asked. "She wasn't going to let you have dad's company. She was using you like she used everyone else."

Unable to look at him any longer, she turned to her father. "I'm sorry," she whispered.

He pulled her into his arms. "You don't have anything to be sorry for. I'm the one who's sorry. I let your mother get away with far too much regarding all of my children."

Once Henry and Robert were led out of the room, EMTs came in to check on Eleanor and Cady. Eleanor had a slight concussion, but otherwise, she would be fine. Cady's only injuries were the red marks on her wrists, a split lip, and a few bruises. Seeing the bruise on her cheek where Henry had backhanded her, Mason and Darrell were ready to rip him apart.

Eleanor happily allowed the EMTs to take her to the hospital, but not before looking at Mason. "I'm sorry," she whispered.

Nodding his head, he hoped she would finally be rid of the demons that had been tormenting her for so long. Not every man was like her ex-husband, not even men who had cheated on their wives. Still holding Melanie, he turned to Cady. "Are you sure you don't need to go to the hospital?"

"I'm fine." She leaned against Darrell. As long as he was holding her, she wasn't going anywhere.

"I'm so sorry you got caught up in my mess," he whispered.

"It's going to be okay now. How did you find me?" Cady looked up at Darrell.

"That was his doing," Darrell nodded at Mason. Before any more explanations could be given, Olivia and Jerrod rushed into the already crowded room. Darrell released Cady so Olivia could pull her into her arms, tears flooding her face.

"I've never been so scared in my life." Pulling slightly

away, she examined her daughter to make sure she was all right. The single bruise on her cheek and split lip caused more tears to roll down her face.

"When you didn't come home from work, I tried to call you. It went straight to voice mail. I thought maybe your plans had changed and you met Darrell instead of coming home first. My heart nearly stopped when he came to pick you up. That's when we realized something was terribly wrong." She was afraid to let go of her daughter after what had just happened.

Standing next to Melanie, Jerrod draped his arm over her shoulders. "How did you get here? I thought you were still in rehab."

Before she could repeat what she'd told her dad, Olivia spoke up. "Can we get out of here? We'll all be more comfortable at the house." She looked at the sheriff with a question in her eyes.

The sheriff nodded at his deputy. "Go ahead, Son. We'll finish up here. I'll need everyone to come to the station tomorrow to give their statements."

Darrell didn't need to be told twice. Still holding Cady close to his side, they filed out of the small room.

Within minutes they were seated in the living room at Olivia's house. "The Jeep has GPS which led us on a wild goose chase," Mason finally answered Cady's earlier question. "It took me longer to remember the key fob also had a GPS chip. When Henry ditched the Jeep, he took the keys with him." He shuddered. "We almost arrived too late." He turned to Melanie. "Why are you here?"

Melanie shrugged. "After you called to check up on me, I knew something was wrong." She looked at Jerrod. "I'm not sure if you noticed, but before Belinda died, she'd been acting weird. Even more weird than usual," she added. "Every time you and Dad were out of town, Grandpa would come over. They would shut themselves in Dad's study doing God only knows what."

She looked at Mason. "I knew they were up to something, but there wasn't anything I could do. I'm sorry I didn't say anything. I was drunk most of the time anyway." She sighed. "After she was gone and Robert took over the hotel here, I realized what she and Grandpa had been planning. I knew I had to make a lot of changes in my life or I was going to end up just like her."

She drew a shuddering breath before going on. "I don't want to be like her. I'm so tired of hating everyone and being hated in return. Do you think you'll ever be able to love me?" Tears streamed down her face at those words. Mason cradled her in his arms, rocking back and forth as though she was a small child.

"Oh, honey, I've always loved you. I wish I could go back and do so many things over. I should have known she was up to something when she pushed so hard for me to let Jerrod run the hotel here. I didn't even know where the site was until it was a done deal."

He looked down at her. "I've apologized to Jerrod and Cady for how I've handled everything. I'm asking for your forgiveness now. I gave up on you when I never should have allowed Belinda to do what she did."

Tears flooded her turquoise eyes. "She always told me you hated me because you hated her and I look like her. I can't change how I look, but I can change how I act."

"I've never hated you," he said quietly. "I simply gave up on you and your brother when I never should have." He looked at Jerrod. "I hope you can both forgive me." He looked at his younger daughter then. "I hope you can also forgive me for allowing Belinda to keep me away from you."

Unable to speak around the lump in her throat, she simply nodded her head. Tears sparkled in her dark eyes where she sat with Darrell.

Melanie looked at Cady and Olivia. "Belinda wanted Jerrod and me to hate both of you. She said you were the reason Dad hated us. But I don't want to hate anyone. I don't want to be hated either. Can we try to get along?"

"I never knew what I was missing by not having a father, but I always wished I had a brother or sister. Now I have all three," Cady answered.

The next morning they met at the sheriff's office to give their statements. The only charges they had against Robert and Henry at the moment were kidnapping and assault on Cady and Eleanor.

With the information Cady was able to give them, Henry would have additional charges of murder, extortion, and conspiracy to commit murder.

"It looks like the old man is aiming for a plea of insanity," Sheriff Taylor told them. He claims his daughter came back from the dead." He looked at Melanie. "I take it that's you."

She nodded her head. "I'm not his dead daughter, I'm his granddaughter. But I do look like her. I hope he doesn't get off because of that. I had to try to stop him from taking over my dad's company. If I had realized he was going to frame him for murder, I would have been here sooner. I'm sorry."

"None of this is your fault, Miss Jarvis." He patted her shoulder as he walked past. "If he does manage to avoid prison with that act, he'll be put in an institution for the criminally insane. I think it's safe to say he isn't going anywhere for a good long time. You all will be called as witnesses when the case comes to trial."

EPILOGUE

Three months later, the small church that Cady and Olivia attended was overflowing with friends and well-wishers. The simple wedding Olivia and Mason had planned somehow turned into an extravaganza. It looked like the entire town had come out for their wedding. Even some of Mason's employees had come to celebrate with them.

After waiting twenty-two years, Olivia was finally marrying the man she'd been in love with for what felt like forever. The term 'the love of her life' was certainly true for her.

Admiring the ring on her finger, butterflies fluttered in Cady's stomach. In two months there will be another wedding. Cady hoped that one wouldn't turn into a circus. *Love at first sight must run in the family*, she thought with a happy smile. *Well, maybe not first sight*, she thought.

Remembering the first time she'd met Darrell she couldn't help but giggle. He thought she'd made up the story that someone was shooting at her so she wouldn't look foolish for walking in the forest in a dress and high heels. But it all worked out in the end.

They were still waiting for Henry's trial. He was pleading insanity, still claiming his dead daughter had come back from the grave. She wasn't sure how that was going to help him. He couldn't claim Melanie had told him to kill Isabell or kidnap Cady. She hoped a jury wouldn't fall for his act the way she had when he pretended to be a kindly homeless man camping out behind the library.

Robert would be spending several years in prison for his role in what had happened. He'd taken a plea on the kidnapping charge. He claimed Henry was the one that shot at Cady. Henry was also the one that killed Isabell. It was a shame Robert had let Belinda and Henry fill him full of wishes

214

and lies. Cady tried to summon up some sympathy for him, but didn't quite make it. He had allowed greed and jealousy to take control of his life. He'd have plenty of time to think about what he should have done differently.

Instead of taking the role of General Manager of the Jarvis House Hotel in Tumbleweed, Jerrod was going to be taking over for his father while Mason and Olivia went on an extended honeymoon. They would be staying at several Jarvis House Hotels as guests, not as owners. Cady thought Jerrod was a good choice to fill his father's shoes while they were gone. They would be back in time for Mason to walk her down the aisle.

Jarvis House Hotels was moving the company headquarters from San Francisco to Tumbleweed. It was a good move for the company and the town. She couldn't decide how she felt about Jerrod moving to Tumbleweed full time. He seemed to enjoy teasing her about everything.

They were also converting the Jarvis House Hotel in Tumbleweed to be more like the rest of the chain: a little bit of bed and breakfast in a hotel. It was what made the hotels so unique and successful.

Cady and Melanie were feeling their way around becoming friends. Melanie was still trying to figure out what to do with the rest of her life. For the first time, she was discovering interests beyond being a socialite. The small community college in Tumbleweed had classes for crafts and hobbies that Melanie was taking advantage of. Maybe she'd finally find her niche.

Eleanor had moved to Phoenix to be with her daughter and two grandchildren. Cady said a prayer that she would eventually find the happiness that had eluded her for so long.

"What are you doing standing out here all alone?" Darrell wrapped his arms around her waist, nuzzling her neck. "I can't wait until it's our turn to walk down that aisle."

Turning in his arms, she wrapped her arms around his neck. How did she deserve this wonderful man? Rising on tiptoes, she placed her lips against his in a feather-light kiss. "That makes two of us," she whispered. "Shall we go see what's holding up this party?" Arm in arm, they walked down the hall to where her mom was finishing getting dressed. After waiting for half of her life to marry the man she loved, she wanted everything to be perfect. Cady might not have waited that long to find the man for her, but she understood her mom's wishes.

Just two more months, she thought. Time would fly, but at the same time, it would drag. It's funny how things turned out. Just six months ago, she hadn't known any of these people who had become so important to her. She was ready to see what else God had in store for her.

ACKNOWLEDGEMENTS

I thank God for the imagination He's given me, enabling me to write my books. I am so blessed by all He has given me. Without Him I can do nothing.

My thanks and gratitude also goes to Sandy Roedl, KaTie Jackson, Cece Blue, and Camala Klaus for their suggestions, editing and encouragement.

Ken Shriner, a retired Phoenix Police Detective was kind enough to answer my many questions regarding law enforcement. I'm grateful for his patience with me throughout the whole process. I've taken liberties with the way law enforcement works in an effort to move the story forward.

I'm most grateful to all of those who read my books. Thank you for your support and encouragement. I would enjoy hearing from you.

OTHER BOOKS BY SUZANNE FLOYD

Dear Reader:

Thank you for reading my book. I hope you enjoyed reading it as much as I did writing it. If you enjoyed Back From The Grave, I hope you will leave a review on Amazon and Goodreads. As an independent author, I don't have a publisher to promote my books. Reviews are the lifeblood of independent authors. I hope you will also check out my other books at Amazon.com.

Follow me on Bookbub and Facebook at Suzanne Floyd Author or check out my web page at Suzanne Floyd.com.

Thank you,
Suzanne Floyd

P.S. If you find any errors, please let me know at:
Suzanne.sfloyd@gmail.com. Before publishing, many people
have read this book, but minds can play tricks by supplying
words that are missing and correcting typos.

Thanks again for reading my book.

ABOUT THE AUTHOR

Suzanne is an internationally known author. She was born in Iowa, and moved to Arizona with her family when she was nine years old where she still lives in Phoenix with her husband, Paul. They have two wonderful daughters, two great sons-in-law and five of the best grandchildren around. Of course, she is just a little prejudiced.

Growing up and traveling with her parents, she entertained herself by making up stories. As an adult she tried writing, but family came first. After retiring in 2008, she decided it was her time. She still enjoys making up stories, and thanks to the internet she's able to put them online for others to enjoy.

When Suzanne isn't writing, she and her husband enjoy traveling around on their 2010 Honda Goldwing trike. She's always looking for new places to write about. There's a new mystery and a romance lurking out there to capture her attention.

Made in the USA
Columbia, SC
20 February 2022

56121420R00124